*What Readers Are ~~Saying about~~ Rusty
Bradshaw's Books:*

The Rehabilitation of Miss Little

Captivating!!

This story is very well written! Rusty does such a great job describing the scenario, he doesn't suck you in - he absorbs you! You feel like you are among the characters. And you have to keep reading to find out what drives the people to do what they are doing. I hope Rusty keeps writing! I look forward to reading another book by him!

Awesome book!

This book was highly recommended to me, so I bought it, I'm so glad I did! I'm not much of a reader, but this book was hard to put down, it kept my attention from start to finish. It's a great story, kind of sad of what she went through, but a good ending. I can hopefully look forward to more books from this author!

Moist on the Mountain

Awesome!

Another good book from the author! Love his writing. I got the book for me, finished it in a couple of days, I was so interested in the story, it was hard to put down.

Fun book to read

Keeps you interested and didn't want to put the book down until finished.

Gorge Justice

Wow! Just wow!

This story was very well written and kept my interest all the way through! Excellent story. I look forward to Rusty's next work of art!

The Best 1 Yet

As I've said before, I'm not a reader, but after reading the first two books from Rusty Bradshaw, I thought I'd read the third. This book is his best yet, I finished it in three days! It made me cry, made me sad, get angry and happy. It's worth reading!!

Excellent reading...

I couldn't put this book down once I started reading it. I was with the character the whole way and hoped that she would finally get justice. Rusty did an excellent job in writing this because you could feel yourself in the surroundings that he described and picture the beautiful scenery. You will not be disappointed in purchasing this book. It is unthinkable what the main character went through and it will keep you on the edge of your seat!

Battle for Stephanie

Kept my interest

Very interesting story, kept me interested til the end! I have read all of Rusty's books and I have enjoyed every one of them, I can't wait til the next one. keep em' coming!

Death in Hazard

Rusty Bradshaw

Dawn,
you will
enjoy this
story!

Rusty Blur (signature)

This book is dedicated to my grandfather, Jesse Moore, the best father figure I had in my life. You will find his name as a character in this book.

Disclaimer:

This is a work of fiction. All of the characters, names, incidents, organizations and dialogue in this work are either the products of the author's imagination or are used fictitiously.

This story was inspired by the song "Hazard," written, produced and performed by singer-songwriter Richard Marx.

Chapter 1

A loud bang jolted Curtis Herden fully awake. He sat up in his single bed in the small bedroom. He blinked his eyes a couple of times to clear the blurriness of sleep. He sat still for a few seconds until a dull thud made him flinch. Then he heard a loud, angry voice.

It was Logan Delgado, his stepfather.

Curtis threw back the covers and swung his legs over the right side of the bed, his feet not quite touching the floor. It was cold in the room, colder than normal. He sat still for a few moments, listening for more sounds. He heard them.

There were more dull thuds. He recognized the sound. He had heard it all too often in the past two years. His mother, Bonnie, was getting slammed against the wall by his stepfather. He heard Delgado's voice interspersed between the thuds. He spoke in a mixture of English and Spanish.

"The pequeno bastardo is a cono," he yelled. "You spoil him too much."

"It was his…." Bonnie started to say, but she was cut off by the hard snap Curtis recognized as a slap to her face.

"He needs to learn to be a hombre," Delgado said. "I need to teach him."

Curtis heard his mother get thrown to the floor and Delgado's heavy footfalls getting louder.

"No," Bonnie screamed. "You leave him alone."

Curtis heard his mother scramble to her feet then run away from his room. It sounded like she was going to the kitchen. The door to his bedroom burst open and Delgado staggered in. He stood about five feet away from where Curtis sat on his bed, but even at that distance, the boy could smell the alcohol seeping through the man's pores. That, too, had become an all too familiar sensation.

Since marrying his mother two years ago, Curtis, even at his young age, recognized that Delgado was a drunk. The physical abuse of his mother started only a couple of months into the marriage, even when Delgado was sober, but it was worse when he was drunk.

Curtis had not suffered any physical abuse from Delgado, but the stepfather was prone to yell at him a lot. That did not help the boy develop a strong self-esteem, especially after what he had experienced in the eighteen months before his mother married Delgado.

Bonnie had married Vince Herden two years before Curtis was born. They had known each other in high school in Centennial, a small Wyoming town. She had ambitions of going to college, although she was undecided on a career path.

But her family, though not dirt poor, did not have the funds to pay for the entirety of her college education. While she was a good student, Bonnie did not receive any scholarships, and government-sponsored financial aid was a route she did not want to take. Because she was uncertain about what she wanted for a career, she did not want to take the risk of not having a job that would allow her to pay back the student loans.

After high school graduation, she got a job with an oil company in the area in the human resources department. Vince had gone to work for the same company, and they saw each other on the job occasionally and eventually started dating. A year after high school, they were married, and two years later, Curtis was born.

His birth brought them even closer together. But there was some sorrow to the event. Bonnie's parents did not live long enough to see their first grandchild. They were both killed in a tragic flight accident shortly after Bonnie's high school graduation.

For the next four years, they both continued their jobs with the oil company. Their idea was to save as much money as they could to eventually fund Bonnie's college education. Working in the human resources office for the oil company helped Bonnie decide this was the direction she wanted her career to go. She had visions of becoming an HR manager some day.

But oil production was declining in the fields where the company was drilling and there had been constant rumors of layoffs, and of the company even pulling up stakes and moving to another state. By the time Curtis was four, they had nearly saved enough money to get Bonnie enrolled at the University of Wyoming.

Shortly after Curtis' fourth birthday, the bottom fell out of their lives.

When her supervisor came to her cubicle that fateful April day, Bonnie could tell there was something wrong.

"What is it, Gretchen?" Bonnie asked.

"There was an accident at your husband's rig," Gretchen Mitchell answered after a pause, trying to find the right words.

Bonnie felt faint. She put her hands on her desk to steady the dizziness.

"How bad is he hurt?" she asked.

Gretchen's face went pale as a ghost.

"I'm sorry, Bonnie. He died," Gretchen said with tears streaming down her cheeks. She reached out and put her hand on Bonnie's shoulder. But Bonnie barely heard her supervisor's words. She knew what they would be before they were spoken. She felt Gretchen's hand on her shoulder, then everything went black.

"Stand up," Delgado shouted.

Curtis hesitated briefly, then slowly slid off the bed facing broadside to his stepfather. Once his feet were solidly on the floor, he dived to the floor directly away from Delgado and rolled under the bed. There was just enough room between the floor and bed for him. With the bed against one wall, Curtis scooted until he was touching it.

"You pequeno pinchazo!" Delgado hollered, then dropped to his knees beside the bed, then he lay on his left side. He reached as far under the bed as he could. But at only five feet six inches, his arms were long enough only to touch Curtis with his fingertips.

"You leave him alone!" Curtis heard his mother scream as she ran into the room.

The boy then heard something that sounded like someone plunging a butcher knife into a watermelon. Delgado screamed, pulled his arm out from under the bed and rolled onto his back. Curtis heard the watermelon sound again. He turned his head so he could see and heard the sound again. This time, he saw a large knife being pulled from Delgado's chest. The eight-inch blade was covered to the handle with blood, and as the knife hovered above him, the semi-thick liquid dripped down onto Delgado's chest.

Curtis heard Delgado breathing, but it was not normal. When he drew a breath in, he wheezed loudly, and there was a bubbling sound like when Curtis blew through a straw into his glass of soda. The same bubbling sounded when he exhaled, and blood started to trickle from the corner of his mouth and slowly run down his cheek.

Time seemed to stop, and the only sounds were Delgado's struggles to get air into his body.

"Oh my God," Bonnie said softly, breaking the silence. Then louder, "Oh my God!"

She dropped the knife, and it fell next to Delgado's left arm, lying flat on the floor after leaving a little slice in the flesh as it fell.

"Curtis, come out," Bonnie instructed.

He slowly edged his way to where Delgado lay next to his bed. The small man was so close to the bed Curtis could not get out without climbing over him. The boy hesitated.

"He's in the way," he told his mother.

Bonnie was frozen in place. The horrifying scene in front of her would not let her think past what she had just done.

"Mom, I can't get out," Curtis said. But she did not respond. He decided he had no choice.

Curtis squeezed between Delgado and the bed frame. It was a tight fit, and he felt the blood from the nearly lifeless body saturate his pajama top. He came out from under the bed and found himself on top of Delgado, facing him. The terror and desperation in the dying man's eyes triggered something in the boy. He felt his hand touch the knife handle on the floor.

What was triggered in him was rage. He had seen this Latino man beat his mother so many times over the years, and he had always wanted to be able to do something to stop it. The rage was mixed with guilt for his inability to protect his mother. The anger and guilt got adrenaline pumping through his small body. His hand tightened around the knife handle. He brought it up and wrapped his other hand around it, the blade pointing down.

Still laying on Delgado's body, he raised the knife over his head. He heard his mother yell, "No, Curtis!" and, at the same time, saw the look of surprise and sheer terror in Delgado's eyes. That look gave him a feeling of satisfaction and he plunged the knife downward and it slid neatly into the man's throat just under his chin. The downward plunge came to an abrupt stop when the tip of the knife hit Delgado's spine.

Blood spurted out, and Curtis felt it splatter on his face. At the same time, he felt his mother grab both his shoulders and yank him backward. He still had a tight grip on the knife and the backward motion pulled it out of the throat wound. More blood squirted out. Delgado took one last gurgling breath and was then silent. His wide-open eyes stared at the ceiling, and his mouth gaped open.

Bonnie began to drag Curtis from the room. But the adrenaline in his little body was still at its peak. As his feet were dragged past the dead man's waist, Curtis planted his left foot firmly on the floor to stop his backward motion. The sudden stop made Bonnie lose her grip on the boy and she fell backward on her butt.

Curtis raised his right foot and slammed it down on Delgado's crotch. He repeated the motion four times before Bonnie could grab his shoulders again and drag him from the room.

"Asshole!" Curtis yelled as he was dragged through the doorway of his bedroom, still clutching the blood-saturated butcher knife. He did not know his parting word fell on deaf ears, and his five stomps to the nuts were not felt by his stepfather. Unfortunately, he knew it was too little too late to protect his mother from the abuse she had already suffered.

Chapter 2

Bonnie was devastated by Vince's death. She had loved him dearly, and before Curtis was born, he had been her whole world.

But her devastation went beyond that.

The circumstances of the accident at the rig that killed her husband were grizzly and shocking. He had been near the well head doing some maintenance on an electrical panel when the alarm sounded that indicated the mud pressure was suddenly building up. Protocol dictated workers to clear the area around the well head in case there was a blowout.

Several workers about fifty yards from the base of the rig said they saw Vince start to run away from the rig when the well head exploded. The mixture of oil and natural gas shot straight up in the air to a height estimated at about four-hundred feet. Because the mixture did not ignite into a fire, workers could see Vince laying on the ground a few feet away from the well head. They started toward him to get him away from the rig, but were called back by the shift supervisor.

"Get back," he yelled. "We can't risk anyone else getting hurt if that oil ignites."

The workers stopped dead in their tracks, then retreated. Through a set of binoculars, the supervisor saw no movement from Vince. Although the body was quickly being covered with oil as it fell back to earth after reaching its peak, the supervisor also saw Vince's head seemed to be separate from his body.

"Oh shit!" he said.

The pocket of oil the drillers were trying to extract turned out to be smaller than they expected, and the geyser of oil diminished to that of a small city park fountain within a few hours. An emergency response team arrived first thing the next morning and capped the well. That allowed crews to recover Vince's body.

It was recovered in two parts. The head was about two feet away from the torso. When the two parts were cleaned up, the medical examiner determined much of the back left side of his head was crushed inward by what the doctor speculated was a flying piece of equipment. The force of the blow tore his head from his body.

The medical examiner recommended Bonnie not view the body, but instead identify her husband from photographs taken in such as way as to not show the worst of the damage. But she insisted.

"I want to see him," she said. "I want to say goodbye to him, not pictures of him."

As much as she tried to prepare herself from the vague descriptions she had been given, seeing her husband's shattered head and scarred body was more than she expected. She became dizzy and nauseated when the drawer at the morgue was pulled out. The ME's aide helped her out of the room and gave her a stainless steel pan to vomit into.

It was an image she would never get out of her mind.

Several months passed before the formal investigation into the well head explosion was concluded. It was determined two major factors led to the disaster that killed Vince, but miraculously spared all others at the rig from death or even injury.

A flaw in the monitoring equipment that was undetected delayed the alarm to signal the mud pressure buildup until the last second. The blowout preventer at the well head was also found to have a crack in the metal that weakened it. When the oil and gas reached the preventer, it blew it apart. One large chunk is what struck Vince in the back of the head as he desperately ran away from the rig.

With Vince gone, Bonnie lost the motivation she had to go to college and pursue a career in human resources. They had saved enough money for her to enroll and get started, but without Vince's presence and encouragement, it didn't seem possible or even worth it.

Then there were the finances.

The combination of the decline of oil production and the well head failure caused the company to shut down operations at the Albany County rig. That meant Bonnie was out of a job.

She and Vince had bought a house in Albany, a small town almost due south of Centennial, just months before the accident. Vince had a life insurance policy through the company, but collecting the money was taking time. It was further delayed because the company was facing its own financial issues due to the circumstances, and bankruptcy was a strong possibility. She had to use money from her college savings to keep herself and her son in their home. She also had to siphon funds from there to pay the utilities and put food on the table.

With the financial shortcomings, Bonnie could not afford the mortgage on the house she and Vince had purchased. She sold it and moved into a rental home. What she got in the home sale barely covered the loan payoff, leaving only a few hundred dollars to add to her bank account.

Because he worked in a high-risk business, Vince had talked with Bonnie about what to do if he were killed on the job. He was adamantly opposed to cremation, which would have been the less expensive approach. Bonnie would not go against her husband's wishes, even though it would have saved her thousands of dollars.

Three months after the accident, Bonnie got a job waiting tables in a local restaurant. But it wasn't enough to cover the rent and all other living expenses, and she continued to drain the savings that had been intended for her college education.

She had been reluctant to look for another romantic relationship after her husband's death. First, because it was too soon, and second, because she did not want to dishonor him. But there came a point when she decided she needed to get more income into the household. That left her two options – getting another or more jobs, or start dating. Part-time jobs were hard to find in the small Wyoming town, especially when she had a young son to raise.

She believed the only option was to find someone to move in with her, and maybe even marry, to share in the household expenses.

Pickings were slim in Albany, and Centennial, its neighbor to the north. Most of the people in the small towns were either married or in committed relationships. Some of the remaining men were much older or younger than Bonnie, and she did not want to get involved with anyone when there was a large age gap. Nor was she interested in a lesbian relationship.

Bonnie was an attractive woman. Her oval face was framed by strawberry blond hair that curled and waved like the breakers on a sandy beach. Her almond-shaped eyes were close set. The unique color of those eyes made it appear she had two emeralds embedded in her face, but they also sometimes had the hue of algae. Her button nose hovered over a small mouth with lips protruding out only slightly. Her rose-beige skin was smooth as glass. At the left corner of her mouth was a mole, only slightly darker than her skin tone, and looked as if someone marked her with a fine-tip Sharpie.

One could describe her figure as hour glass. But it was an hour glass that allowed time to pass faster than normal. If the saying about women's breasts were true – more than a handful is a waste – Bonnie's nearly fit the bill, allowing only a small amount of waste. Standing five feet three inches, she was a compact woman.

Bonnie met and dated several men. But the first two balked at any further contact when they learned she had a young child. Both were young business owners, one in Albany and the other in Centennial. They both told her they did not want to raise someone else's child.

She dated one man for a week, and things looked promising. He was a few years older than Bonnie, but things between them were going so well she was willing to entertain a relationship with him.

But then she discovered he had a criminal record and had actually spent a few years in the Wyoming State Penitentiary in

Rawlins for assault, having been released just months earlier. She ended their association, but he persisted until she filed a restraining order against him.

She tried a few more times, but each time, there was something that told her it would not work.

Then she met Logan Delgado, a suave, slightly dark-skinned man who gave the appearance of being a Latino. He drove for a local trucking company. He was very polite, only one year younger than Bonnie, and he treated her like a queen. He seemed to have an endless amount of money, and he spent it lavishly on her. He seemed to have no problem that she had a young boy, and five-year-old Curtis appeared comfortable with him.

Bonnie never saw Delgado take a drink of alcohol and he was not a smoker. Cleanliness was important to him and he dressed well.

They dated for two months. In that time, they got along very well. While they disagreed on some things from time to time, there was never a cross word spoken between them.

One Saturday night, he took her to the best restaurant in Albany. They enjoyed a meal of top sirloin steaks, baked potatoes and mixed vegetables. Their dinner conversation was of everyday things – how his day went, how Curtis was doing in school, how things were going with her part-time job.

After they finished a dessert of peach pie al-la-mode, Delgado stood and moved to the side of her chair, dropped to one knee and took her hand. Bonnie's heart skipped a beat because she knew what this gesture meant. Delgado took a small felt-covered box from his pocket and opened it. Inside was a simple silver band with a small diamond within an ornate setting.

"Bonnie, will you marry me?" he asked.

She felt her body temperature rise a few degrees, especially in her cheeks that took on a reddish tone.

Bonnie's mind raced, trying to go over all the reasons to say yes or no. She was concerned that she had only known this man for two months, and while they had conversed many times, she still knew little about his background. She still did not know where he was from nor anything about his family. She was also concerned that Delgado seemed to have more money than a trucker would make. There were a number of other things that gave her pause.

But in the end, she made the only decision that made sense for her survival and that of her son.

Chapter 3

Delgado, Bonnie and Curtis drove to Laramie, the Albany County seat, one early spring day to obtain a marriage license. In a month when the trees were normally starting to green up and wildflowers were beginning to sprout in most places, it was still winter in Wyoming. The road to Laramie was slushy with recently melted snow, and the fields on either side were white as far as the eye could see.

It was not the best time to be traveling, but Delgado had insisted. In his sophisticated and alluring way, he convinced Bonnie that there was no time like the present.

"Mi amor, I love you so much. I want to be with you always," he cooed. "If I have to wait any longer, I don't know if I could stand it."

Bonnie was leery at first. In the time they had been dating, Delgado had made numerous sexual advances toward her. But she was unwilling to take that step with him. She was afraid; all he wanted was to get into her pants. She had experienced that already with a couple of the men she had dated.

Because of that, she had made it clear to Delgado that there would be no sex between them unless there was a long-term commitment. After all, she and Vince had not had sexual intercourse until after they were married. If he could wait, so could anyone else, she told Delgado.

"I understand completely, mi preciosa," he said. "I totally agree."

She hesitated, remembering the times he had tried to initiate sex with her since they met.

"I know I have pushed a little bit, mi reina," he said. "But you are just so hermosa I could not help myself."

Seeing her relax a little, he bored right in.

"I want you for mi esposa, for the rest of my life," he said. "I am so proud of you, and I can't wait to tell people I am your papi."

Having grown up in rural Wyoming, Bonnie had never yet been farther away from the state than northern Colorado and western Nebraska; she found Delgado to be exotic. Sprinkling Spanish words within his speech only enhanced that for Bonnie. And despite her desire to be very careful in choosing another mate, she was mesmerized by his Latin charm.

She finally gave in, and they were on the road. Curtis was with them on the drive to Laramie because Delgado told her he wanted the boy to be fully involved in the new family they were creating. He told her he had no children and wanted to have a family.

"I would like, with your permission and his, to adopt him some day," Delgado had said.

That convinced Bonnie there was another layer of commitment Delgado was willing to accept. That was the final piece to the puzzle, as far as Bonnie was concerned.

For his part, Curtis, who was just barely five years old, there was no real investment. The memory of his father, as short and faint as it was, remained in his mind. He was not ready to have that memory wiped away by another man.

But despite his youth, Curtis could see how worried and stressed his mother was having to raise and financially support him on her own, and conversely, how she seemed to brighten up when the prospect of marrying Delgado became more of a reality. He resigned himself to the developing new family and decided he would do his part to make the best of it, for his mother's sake if not his own.

It did not take long for Delgado to show his true colors. But it wasn't like Bonnie had no warnings.

She had been friends with Lauralei Munson since high school. She was there for Bonnie after Vince died, inviting her and Curtis to stay at her home for the first couple of weeks after the death to help her adjust. That gave them plenty of time to talk, as Lauralei was single at the time.

After those first weeks following her first husband's death, Bonnie returned to her newly rented home to try and settle into a new normal. Lauralei visited often and that helped ease the shock of now living in a home without her husband, who would never be a part of her life again.

When Bonnie decided to start dating, Lauralei tried to dissuade her. But she could see that Bonnie was determined, and Lauralei knew that part of the reason was financial. Failing to change her mind about jumping back into the dating pool, Bonnie's friend then tried to help by steering her away from certain types of men. However, Lauralei's "certain type" of men included nearly all of them.

"Men are after only one thing," she told Bonnie on more than one occasion. "Once they have that, you become just their plaything. You'll only matter when they're horny."

"But Vince wasn't like that at all," Bonnie countered. "He was loving and caring. He never mistreated me."

Lauralei, a tall, long-legged, attractive brunette, knew that was true. She had adored Vince, even hoping when they were both still in high school that she might marry him some day. But once he married Bonnie, she left all those desires behind and she was overjoyed for her friend.

"I've met a few guys, and they seem very nice," Bonnie said.

"Yeah, but you can't trust men," Lauralei said. "They'll use tons of charm to get you interested, then pour it on until they get you hooked. But once they have you reeled in, it's like all that charm goes right back into the bait bucket."

Lauralei knew of what she spoke. She had the misfortune of choosing two men just like that. She had married each of them. But both marriages lasted less than a year. When each husband turned into an unloving, uncaring slob that treated her like his personal slave – sex and otherwise – she wasted no time in getting a quicky divorce each time.

She saw her friend falling into the same trap when she started seeing Delgado. But her intensified warnings fell on deaf ears.

The truth came crashing down on Bonnie – figuratively and literally – just one month into her new marriage. Delgado came home late one night and he was three sheets to the wind.

"Where's my dinner, bruja?" he yelled as he stumbled through the front door.

Bonnie was taken aback. She had never seen him behave this way. She knew he drank alcohol, but up to now, she had only seen him imbibe in moderation.

"It's in the fridge," Bonnie answered hesitantly, suddenly on the defensive. "You weren't here at dinner time so I saved it for you. You didn't call to let me know you were going to be late or when you would be home."

"Do you think I need to report to you every move I make?" Delgado spat, getting nose-to-nose with her. "You're not my madre."

Bonnie eased away from him and went to the refrigerator to get the plate covered with plastic wrap. Delgado's swinging arm caught the plate as Bonnie slowly turned from the fridge toward the microwave. The plate went flying, and when it hit the cabinet door above the stove, the plastic wrap let loose its grip and the steak, mashed potatoes and corn scattered throughout the kitchen.

"Not that leftover mierda. Make me something fresh," he hollered, then went in and plopped down in the recliner.

With no meat thawed out, Bonnie didn't know what to make for the man she suddenly did not know. He was facing away from the kitchen in the recliner, so she took the steak from where it lay on the counter, chopped it up and put it in a frying pan just enough to warm it up. She then made some Spanish rice and refried beans. Once it was all done, she mixed some hot sauce into the meat and warmed two corn tortillas.

When she took the plate to Delgado, he just motioned for her to put it on the end table.

"Now go clean up that damned mess you made," he said.

That made Bonnie's blood boil. The mess "you" made indeed. She wanted to tell him to go clean it himself, since it was, in fact, he who made the mess. But the shock of his behavior and the outburst in the kitchen made her afraid to speak up, lest she provoke a more violent outburst that could bring injury upon herself or her son.

So, she meekly turned and picked up all the food remnants and wiped down the counter, cabinet and floor.

When she was done, she took a few steps toward the living room, but she stopped in her tracks when she heard rattled breathing coming from the area of the recliner. She slowly walked around it to see Delgado sound asleep with his head tilted toward his left shoulder and drool rolling out of the corner of his mouth. She glanced at the end table and saw the dinner plate she had made for him untouched where she had left it.

Her anger rose up again. But she stifled it and went to bed, finding sleep hard to find. After getting maybe two hours of restless shut-eye, she woke to a house as quiet as a church during silent prayer. She got up to check on things, finding Curtis sound asleep in his bed. In the living room, the recliner was empty, and the dinner plate she made Delgado the night before remained, untouched, on the end table. He was nowhere in the house.

For a week after that first outburst by Delgado, he returned to the charming personality he displayed while he and Bonnie were dating. But now she was on alert. She expected the violent side of him to emerge again. When it did, a plate full of food was not upon what he took his drunken anger.

Again, he was out drinking with his buddies, and when he came home, Bonnie was already in bed, sound asleep. With the memory of that first inebriated entrance the week before, she didn't bother leaving him a plate of food. What was the point? He wouldn't eat it, just scatter it all over the place in another outburst and leave her to clean up the mess.

When Delgado stumbled into the house that night, he saw no one waiting up for him. That was irritating to him because despite the alcohol he had consumed – and probably because of it – he was horny. In the first three weeks of his marriage to Bonnie, they had sex several times per week. She had insisted on waiting until they were married before they consummated the relationship, and Delgado had gritted his teeth and obeyed. But after the courthouse wedding, he made up for it. Bonnie initially went along the first few times. They were husband and wife, after all, and she was no prude. But the sheer frequency was more than she really wanted.

Not that Delgado was a bad lover. He was gentle, caring and attentive to her needs the first few times. But then it became increasingly more about his needs, and he became rougher. Bonnie didn't mind a little aggressive lovemaking, but in the last week before Delgado's drunken tirade, it became so rough that she developed a few bruises.

And for the week since that violent evening, she had not allowed him to even fondle her. He was frustrated, she could tell, but he didn't make an issue out of it, at least not outwardly. Within, he let it fester.

While out drinking with his friends, he let it slip through his alcoholic haze that he wasn't getting any. That brought on a lot of ribbing, and they questioned his manhood. That did not set well with the macho persona he tried to project. Delgado went home that night bound and determined to get himself some pussy.

Finding Bonnie not waiting for him when he got home further stoked the fire smoldering in his belly. He stomped to the bedroom and flung open the door. It slammed against the door stopper and that brought Bonnie awake with a jolt.

He had turned the living room light on and left it that way and his figure was silhouetted in the bedroom doorway. She knew it was her husband by the build, but somehow, that knowledge did not diminish the fear that made her heart race when she heard the door slam open.

"It's time for you to be a wife, perra," Delgado slurred, then started removing his clothing.

Bonnie, now sitting straight up in bed, did not move, not even a twitch. Delgado had removed his shirt and kicked off his boots. He was in his jeans, socks and tank top undershirt and took a few steps toward the bed.

"Get that nightgown off," he said when he saw Bonnie hadn't made a move. She grabbed the blankets and pulled them up tight to her throat.

"It's time for you to stop being a torturador de pinchazo," he hollered as he quickly half fell on the bed over Bonnie and pushed her down onto the pillows.

She held tight to the blankets and kept them covering her body. Delgado tried to pull them away, but Bonnie held them close, and there was no give. He raised his arm and balled his fist, bringing it crashing into Bonnie's left cheek. His blow landed with surprising force, considering his condition. Bonnie screamed but didn't let go of the blankets. But when the fist came in again and smashed into her left ear, she released her grip on the blankets with her left hand to bring it to her ringing and painful ear. That was the opening Delgado needed, and he jerked the blankets away.

Bonnie was still smarting from the two blows to the head, she hadn't even been able to wipe the trickle of blood from her nose, and Delgado ripped her nightgown open, exposing her breasts. He grabbed each and squeezed, then bent his face down and began sucking on one nipple. Bonnie regained her senses and started slapping his head. This time Delgado's punch was to her abdomen, and it took the wind right out of her.

With his wife gasping for breath, Delgado went on with his assault on her tits, sucking and biting both nipples alternatively. When Bonnie was just catching her breath, Delgado reached both hands down and yanked her panties down to her ankles. Bonnie's instinctive reaction was to place her hands over her public area. Delgado came down with both fists on her shoulders, and Bonnie threw her hands up to them in an attempt to sooth the pain, which was futile.

Delgado then unfastened his pants and pulled them and his underwear down as far as he could get them. He then slammed his erect penis into her unguarded and relaxed vagina. She had no time to react and tighten the entrance with her groin muscles. Delgado started to thrust in and out quickly. After only a few pumps, Bonnie felt his ejaculate inside her, and he tensed, and his hardon emptied its load. He then collapsed on top of her. Within seconds, he was snoring.

She lay there for almost a full minute, his dead weight pushing down on her and making her breathing difficult. She finally slowly pushed up on his shoulders and rolled him over to the other side of the bed. She again lay still for a minute to make sure he was still asleep. She then got out of bed, her tattered nightgown still open at the front. She stepped her feet out of her underwear, picked them up and headed for the half bath off the kitchen. Along the way she peeked into Curtis' room and found him sound asleep.

Or so it seemed. Because he was a light sleeper, the noise from the master bedroom woke him up. Despite his worry, Curtis was too afraid to go investigate. Afraid of what he might find and afraid of what Delgado might do to him. When the noise finally stopped, and he heard the master bedroom door open, he feigned sleep.

After Bonnie had looked in on Curtis, she cleaned herself from head to toe then threw both the night gown and underwear in the kitchen trash bin. She tiptoed back to the master bedroom where Delgado's rhythmic snoring assured her he was still asleep. Bonnie grabbed a sweatshirt and sweatpants from her dresser, slipped them on and went to the living room.

She was still asleep on the couch when Delgado got up in the morning. He didn't give her a second look as he headed out the door for work.

Not much changed in the next couple of years. There were more beatings, and Delgado took advantage of her sexually frequently. After a few months, she stopped fighting his advances, but that didn't stop his violence against her.

But in that time, he had never laid a hand on Curtis, and Bonnie was thankful for that. She even came to think that if she gave herself willingly to him, that would help protect her son.

While he never struck Curtis, he eventually yelled at him from time to time for trivial digressions, or sometimes for no reason at all that she could see. Bonnie could tell her husband resented the boy for some reason. It was something she could not put her finger on, but Delgado's disdain for Curtis was easy to read on his face.

Curtis was concerned when he saw his mother's black eye from the night of Delgado's assault upon her. When he asked what happened, Bonnie simply told him she tripped and hit her head on one of the dressers in her bedroom. He overtly accepted the explanation without question. But he knew there was more to it, and he could guess what.

After that incident, whether he was drunk or sober, Delgado was careful in all the other beatings of his wife to strike her in places that would not show when she was dressed. But Curtis sometimes heard the hollering and recognized the sounds when his stepfather struck his mother. He wanted to do something to stop the assaults on her, but he was afraid. He feared not just getting beaten himself, but would any actions he took make it worse on his mother? He kept it to himself, and it festered.

Delgado's death came on the night of Curtis' seventh birthday. While her husband was at work, Bonnie took Curtis to Laramie for a shopping trip. She wanted to allow him to pick his own presents. He selected a Wyoming Cowboys T-shirt and cap they found at a department store. She then took him to dinner at a child-themed fast food restaurant where he was able, after eating all his meal, to enjoy some time on the restaurant's indoor playground.

Later that night, when Delgado came home late once again after a few drinks with his pals, he saw the shirt in the laundry area on the back porch and demanded to know where it came from.

"I took Curtis shopping in Laramie and then to a restaurant," she told him.

"Why the hell do that? We can't afford crap like that," he slurred.

"But it was his birthday," she pleaded. "I wanted to do something special for him."

Delgado drew back his arm and sent the back of his hand crashing into her face. It knocked her backward, but she stayed on her feet.

"The pequeno bastardo is a cono," he yelled. "You spoil him too much."

"It was his… " Bonnie started to say, but she was cut off by the hard snap Curtis recognized as a slap to her face.

"He needs to learn to be a hombre," Delgado said. "I need to teach him."

That is when he stalked toward Curtis' room and Bonnie ran to the kitchen.

Chapter 4

Bonnie sat quietly in a walk-in closet size interview room in the Albany County Jail in Laramie. She was nervous about what was going to happen to her. But even more, she was worried about what was going to happen to Curtis if she went to prison for killing her husband. Strangers would probably take in the seven-year-old boy, and Bonnie was concerned that the incident in their Albany home would mentally scar her son in a way that only she could find ways to heal.

After all, she was his mother, and no stranger could possibly fill those shoes.

She had no idea where Curtis was or what was happening to him. After forcing him to leave the bedroom where Delgado stared blankly at the ceiling, she called 911 and told the dispatcher there was a death at her home, and she gave the address.

"My husband is dead," she said when asked what happened.

"Is he breathing?" the dispatcher asked.

"I don't think so," Bonnie replied.

"How do you know he is dead?" was the dispatcher's next question.

"I just know," Bonnie said.

"Officers are on their way," the dispatcher said. "It might be a while because the county deputies are coming from a few miles away. But I need you to stay on the line with me."

Bonnie, with Curtis clutched to her chest, slowly lowered the cell phone to the floor and used both arms to hug her son tighter. She began to sob. But Curtis made no sound at all.

"Hello, ma'am, are you still there?" the dispatcher asked.

Bonnie made no attempt to respond, but left the phone connection open. The dispatcher prompted her several more times but got no response.

"I think the connection is still open, but she won't respond," Bonnie heard the dispatcher say to someone in the call center. Bonnie reached down and put the call with the 911 operator on hold. She picked up the phone and scrolled through her contacts to find Lauralei's number and pushed the call button.

"Hey, girl, what's up?" her friend's cheery voice chirped through the phone. As late as it was, Bonnie was surprised Lauralei had answered so quickly and was so upbeat. She was sure she would have woken her up from a sound sleep. It threw Bonnie off, and she didn't respond.

"Bonnie, you there? What's happening?" Lauralei asked with a touch of concern, breaking up her happy-sounding mood.

"Something bad has happened at home," Bonnie finally managed.

"Bon, what happened?" her friend asked.

"It is very bad," she said.

"I'll be right there," Lauralei said and hung up before Bonnie could say another word.

Lauralei lived on the far side of town, but it seemed to Bonnie that her friend burst through the front door just as she ended the call and took the 911 operator off hold. But at one o'clock in the morning, with the streets deserted in the small town, she had screamed through town at more than seventy miles per hour.

"...you there? Ma'am, I need you to talk to me," the dispatcher's voice came through in mid-sentence. Lauralei kneeled at Bonnie's side just as the dispatcher repeated her plea for the caller to speak to her. Lauralei picked up the phone and said hello.

"Who is this?" the dispatcher asked.

"I am Bonnie's friend Lauralei. I just got here after she called me," she responded.

"What happened there?" the dispatcher asked.

Lauralei looked at Bonnie, who was staring down the short hallway in the direction of the bedrooms, flanking the shared bathroom. Lauralei picked up Bonnie's cell phone and stood up.

"Give me a minute to look around," she responded. "She hasn't told me anything, but she is really scared. She and her son have blood on their clothes and faces."

"Your friend said there was a death in the house. Be careful and try to touch as little as you can in case this turns into a crime scene," the dispatcher instructed.

Both bedroom doors were open but there were no lights on in either room. Lauralei went first to the master bedroom doorway. In the darkened room, she could make out the different shapes that identified the furniture inside. She carefully reached inside the room to the left of the doorway. With the sleeve of her sweatshirt covering her hand, she flipped the light switch and retracked her arm.

The bed was in the middle of the room, with the head against the far wall. There were two five-drawer dressers, one in a corner to the left of the bed and the other against the wall opposite the foot of the bed. The bed was neatly made and clearly not yet slept in that night.

Lauralei then stopped at the closed bathroom door. She caught the slightest metallic and sweet order. It was a smell she did not recognize. She slowly turned the bathroom doorknob and opened it enough to reach in and flip the light switch with her covered hand. Ever so slowly, she pushed the door open. But there was nothing unusual in the room.

She then turned to Curtis' room. As she advanced into the doorway, the scent she first noticed became stronger. She again turned the light on with a covered hand. What she saw made her jump back a step.

Delgado lay flat on his back next to Curtis' bed. From where she stood in the hallway, she saw that his eyes were wide open, and there was a look of terror frozen on his face. His undershirt was a dull red, and his neck was also red, but of a brighter hue.

She retreated into the bathroom and vomited in the sink.

"What is happening, Lauralei?" she heard the 911 dispatcher ask with some urgency from the phone still in her hand.

Lauralei retched again, this time into the toilet, at having to recall the grizzly scene in Curtis' bedroom. She used some toilet paper to wipe the slimy barf remnants from her face, then put the phone to her ear.

"My friend's husband is dead; there is blood all over him," she said.

As the last word passed through her lips, she felt the bile rising in her throat again. She leaned over the toilet and expelled what seemed like a gallon of bitter liquid. It also went into her sinus and ran out of her nose.

For about the tenth time, Bonnie went through the whole description of that fateful night, from the time Delgado came home until the deputies arrived at her home. The basic facts of the story she had to tell never wavered, but when she described his death, she did not mention that Curtis was involved in the stabbing.

Several times the detectives interviewing her bored in on that aspect of the night, and she repeated it more times than any other part of the narrative.

"Your son was in the room, correct?" Detective Gerald McWeeny asked as they went over the actual stabbing one more time.

"Yes, he was," Bonnie said. She was exhausted from the ordeal at the house and the six-hour interrogation. But she fought to stay sharp enough to keep her story straight.

"But he did not stab your husband?" the detective asked. He had heard it all multiple times already. But he was looking for any slip in her description.

"He didn't," Bonnie said calmly. "I stabbed him in the chest a few times and then in the neck."

"Why did you stab him in the neck?" Detective Arvin Scheshefski asked. "You didn't think stabbing him in the chest was enough?"

"I don't know," Bonnie responded. "I was angry."

"Because he beat you up from time to time?" Scheshefski asked.

"Yes, and he was going to hurt my son," she answered, then took a long drink of the warm water in a tall glass in front of her.

"Did he ever beat on Curtis during your marriage?" Scheshefski asked.

"No, but he was very mean to him in other ways," she said.

"How was he mean to your son?" McWeeny asked.

"He called him names, he sometimes broke his toys in front of him, he tried to get Curtis mad enough to try and hit him," Bonnie said. "I think he did want to hit Curtis, but wanted to do it in response to something. But Curtis never allowed himself to be provoked."

The two detectives looked at each other. They had used the tactic of alternating who did the questioning in a way that Bonnie would not recognize a pattern and know who would ask the next question. They hoped that would cause her to slip up at some point. But her story stayed the same from the beginning.

But the detectives knew two things that Bonnie did not. During short breaks in their interview of her, they were told that Curtis' fingerprints where on the knife, and Curtis was telling two other detectives that it was he, not his mother, who stabbed Delgado.

His description of the actual stabbing was exactly the same as his mother's, except in his version, he had plunged the knife into his stepfather multiple times, not his mother.

McWeeny and Scheshefski, through their expressions to each other, had decided the time had come to reveal what they knew.

"Okay, Mrs. Delgado, we have…." McWeeny began, but Bonnie cut him off.

"I am not Mrs. Delgado; I'm Bonnie Herden," she said firmly.

"Excuse me," Scheshefski said, as he looked down at her driver's license in front of him. "It says Bonnie Delgado on your ID."

"I'm going back to using my first married name," she said. "I don't want to be associated with that asshole."

Up until this point in the interview, the detectives had referred to her only by her first name, trying to establish some level of friendly connection with her, hoping that would make her feel more at ease and open up to them. But this marked a new direction for the questioning, and the detectives had agreed before they started the interrogation that there would come a time when they would have to be more formal.

Bonnie's declaration, made so suddenly and with conviction, threw both detectives off their game – but only momentarily.

"OK, Mrs. Herden, we'll make a note of that," McWeeny said as he wrote it in his notes.

"Now, we have some information that we have not shared with you," Scheshefski said. "Your son's fingerprints were found on the knife used to stab your husband."

He held back the other bombshell while they waited to get her reaction to this news.

"If you check fingerprints on all the knives in my kitchen, you will probably find his fingerprints on all of them," Bonnie said calmly.

"And why would a seven-year-old boy be handling a butcher knife, steak knives and other things like that?" McWeeny asked.

"He helps me cook sometimes," she answered evenly. "I want him to learn how to cook."

After a few seconds of thought, the detectives plowed on.

"Here's the other thing we know that you don't," Scheshefski said. "Your son is claiming he did all the stabbing, completely opposite of what you are telling us."

McWeeny picked up the narrative before Bonnie could respond.

"He claims Delgado was beating you, and after crawling out from under his bed, he went to the kitchen, got the knife, ran back to his bedroom and stabbed Delgado."

Bonnie's expression did not change even a little bit. It remained as stoic as it had from the beginning of the interview.

"He is trying to protect me," she said.

"And are you trying to protect him?" Scheshefski asked.

"No, I'm telling you exactly what happened," Bonnie responded.

The detectives looked at each other again, exchanging silent messages. They then stood up and headed for the interview room door without saying another word.

McWeeny and Scheshefski walked out of the jail building through a back door. They had been interviewing Bonnie Delgado – now Bonnie Herden, as they had just been informed – for just more than two hours straight in this session. Their nicotine cravings had kicked in about thirty minutes ago.

They both pulled in lungs full of cigarette smoke, held it a few seconds, and then blew out what was left.

"What do you think?" Scheshefski asked.

"I think she did it all herself," McWeeny said without hesitation.

"What takes you to that conclusion?" his partner asked.

"For one thing, I don't believe a seven-year-old has the strength physically to stab a knife that deep into someone's chest," McWeeny explained. "Plus, even if he did somehow, I'm not so sure a seven-year-old would have the stomach to do it again."

The medical examiner's report had not yet been completed, but observation at the scene of the death showed four stab wounds. One was on the right side just above the hip, the second just to the left of center in his chest, the third a few inches below the first chest wound and the fourth dead center to his throat. Each wound, except for the neck, measured the same as the widest part of the butcher knife at the base of the handle. The chest wounds still had the impression of the knife handle around the wound, like someone had made an impression in clay.

"I suppose if his adrenaline was pumping, he could have made the multiple wounds," Scheshefski said. "But I agree with you about the physical strength. That knife was pushed down pretty damned hard to make those impressions."

"Do you think he could have done any one of those wounds?" McWeeny asked.

"I suppose the side wound could have been his, trying to protect his mother while she was being attacked," Scheshefski speculated. "Then the mother could have taken the knife from him and stabbed Delgado."

He took a long drag on his cigarette, which was getting close to the filter.

"Well, if we are agreed that she did the killing, what do we charge her with?" McWeeny asked, puffing at his own cigarette, then dropping it to the pavement and grounding it out with his boot.

"If we go by the book, since there are multiple wounds, and a very vicious one in the neck at that, it would have to be manslaughter at least," Scheshefski said.

McWeeny thought for a moment. He had seen his share of domestic violence cases during his thirteen-year career in Wyoming law enforcement. Even though it was outdated, the machismo attitude of the man being the master of the house and the woman being obedient still cropped up. As the times changed over the years, women began to take more control, even in abusive situations.

McWeeny had worked two such cases in his career in which the man was killed by the abused woman, and both had been within the last two years. He tended to sympathize with women in those situations, believing they were delivering karma to their abusers. But on the other hand, he was concerned that if women got away with, or got slaps on the wrist, for turning to killing their abusers, the wrong message would be sent, and women could turn to murder always in abusive situations. That wasn't right.

"You know I'm on the fence on this call," he told Scheshefski.

His partner nodded as he ground out his cigarette with the toe of his shoe.

"Alright, let's send manslaughter up the flagpole and see what the prosecutor does with it," Scheshefski said.

Chapter 5

Bonnie sat on the thin mattress of the metal bed in the holding cell at the Albany County Jail. The sun, quite bright because it was reflecting off the blanket of snow that had fallen in the hour just before sunrise, shed light through the small window near the top of the wall in the back of the cell.

It wasn't surprising to her that the sun was unfettered by clouds just minutes after a snowfall. There was a saying common in Wyoming – don't like the weather, wait five minutes. Wind is prevalent in the state and pushes climate fronts of varying types through the state rapidly. Despite the cold temperatures that prevail in Wyoming through the winter, chinook winds blow pockets of warmer temperatures ahead of them. That results in brief clear skies and higher temperatures for brief periods.

On this early March morning, Bonnie Herden was trying to understand why she was locked up. She had not slept all night. The events of the previous night and her hours of interrogation by the two Albany County detectives had done little to make it clear. She knew her husband was dead, and she was responsible for it. The memories of the incident in their home were crystal clear in her mind. She could recall every detail with clarity.

But what had driven her to stab Delgado was unclear. After all, she had put up with the abusive and controlling behavior for nearly two years. He had also been filled with contempt for Curtis that entire time and made no secret of his desire to either mold the boy in his image, or find a way to get him out of their lives.

Trying to make sense of it all was the only thing occupying her sleepless mind. Even her own fate held no interest to her. Curtis was now safe from Delgado, what happened to her was of little consequence.

But it was not long before she began to get an education into what was going to happen to her. That information was not the only thing she would learn in the coming weeks.

Bonnie could not afford a top-notch attorney, so ended up with a public defender. But she was fortunate to get Holly Quarters.

She was just one year out of law school at the University of Wisconsin and had made a name for herself in the Albany County legal community as a tenacious, hard-fighting lawyer. In the past year she had defended four clients and won all four cases. She was a master of research. She had to be. There were few resources for investigators in her office. But she was not satisfied relying on law enforcement's investigations.

Holly spent a lot of time, off the clock, at the law library, scouring the Internet and interviewing people. She was a voracious reader, and the lights in her small Laramie apartment burned much of the night as she studied and coordinated her cases.

In other words, she had no social life.

In their first meeting, the day after her incarceration, Bonnie learned that she and Holly had a very important thing in common. Holly had also survived an abusive relationship. In fact, while in her first year in college, she had been stalked and raped by a member of the Wisconsin football team.

An athlete herself in high school, Holly was tall for a woman, more than six feet. She was slender but muscular, and she had an attractive hourglass figure. Her strawberry blond hair was wavy and hung well below her shoulders. Her high cheekbones and petite nose were not the most outstanding features of her face. Her emerald green eyes were like *Star Trek* tractor beams, demanding the attention of those around her.

So, she drew a lot of attention on the Madison campus. One admirer was a Badger linebacker. She rejected his advances because she was, even then, driven to be a successful lawyer and wanted no distractions. But he wouldn't have it and continued to pursue her. Her complaints to campus security and even the Madison Police Department gave her no relief, partly because those department officials did not want to upset the apple cart for the university's football team.

One late night, she was walking back to her dormitory when the football player, about her height but outweighing her by at least seventy pounds, accosted her. When she told him she wanted no part of him, he backhanded her across the face. While she was semi-dazed, he wrapped his arms around her and dragged her behind a hedge that wound around a darkened building.

When her protests gained in volume, though it was late enough that there was no one around to hear her, he grabbed her throat and squeezed while pulling out a switchblade knife and snapped open the six-inch blade.

"You keep your mouth shut, or I'll gut you like a fish," he said.

With the knife between his teeth like a movie pirate, he then unfastened and pulled down her jeans, followed by her panties. He released the grip on her neck and pulled her T-shirt and bra off. Forcing her to the ground, he held her hands together over her head with his left hand while massaging her thirty-six D breasts with the other. After a minute, he put his head against them and began chewing on her nipples. He was not subtle about it, and Holly had to bite her lip to keep from crying out because of the pain.

When he stopped chewing, he pulled down his own jeans and underwear, and Holly felt the head of his cock against the lips of her vagina. He tried pushing it in, but she was tense, and her vagina was dry. The football player took the knife from his mouth and placed it on Holly's neck. He pushed harder, and she felt his hardened penis slip in about halfway. The pain made her groan.

"So, you do like it," he teased.

"You're hurting me," she whispered.

His only response was to push harder, but his member wouldn't budge any further. When he tried to push again, Holly felt his semen enter her.

"Oh God," she muttered.

He left his cock inside her until he shot his wad. Then he pulled it out, stood, pulled up his pants and fastened them. He looked down on her and gave her a mighty kick in the groin. Holly couldn't hold her voice any longer and screamed from the pain. The player took off at a dead run.

Holly lay there long enough to make sure the player was gone. She then got up, redressed and went straight to the hospital.

"I had a rape kit done and then went and filed a complaint with the Madison police," Holly told Bonnie after telling the tale in that first meeting. "They had no choice then, and he was charged and convicted. Still in jail, as far as I know."

While hearing Holly's story, Bonnie flashed back to her marriage to Delgado. She had lost track of the times he had taken advantage of her sexually during the marriage. After he showed his true colors, Bonnie did not want to have sex with him and did so only reluctantly. Other times, she tried to resist, but he always took what he wanted. Her story sounded very much like Holly's, only repeated over and over again.

"But he came inside you. Did you get pregnant?" Bonnie asked.

"No," she answered. "Once the rape kit was done, I douched right there in the hospital – twice. I was lucky."

Bonnie nodded with a mixture of sympathy and relief on her face.

"I told you that because I want you to know that I have a pretty good idea what you have gone through," Holly said. "And I also wanted you to know that that drives me to do the best job I can for you."

As they met over the next few weeks Bonnie saw just how dedicated to her case Holly was.

Curtis continued to stay with Lauralei, and Bonnie's friend visited her in jail multiple times per week to give her updates on her son. Bonnie refused to allow Curtis to visit her in jail, but Holly convinced the court to agree to let Lauralei take videos of her with her phone and play them back for the boy. During these videos, Bonnie tried to be as upbeat as she could. Lauralei also confided to her friend that Curtis continued to try and convince people that he was the one, not his mother, who killed Delgado.

Bonnie had not told even Holly that Curtis had delivered the final stab to Delgado's throat. While the three stabs she had made in his side and chest were severe, the throat wound was the fatal one. She was willing to fall on the sword to save her son from any further trauma.

While that was uppermost on Bonnie's priority list, it was not Holly's.

In the following weeks, the young attorney put her research into high gear while the wheels of justice turned at its normal speed – slowly. Bonnie was arraigned and the judge decided there was enough evidence to take the case to trial. He scheduled it for sixty days hence.

In those two months, Holly found some interesting information that she believed could turn the tables for her client. One of those things had little that was helpful for Bonnie's release from jail. But it was a surprise for her client.

"Did you think you were married to a Latino man?" Holly asked Bonnie during a briefing in a private interview room at the jail complex.

"Well, yeah," she answered. "He knew Spanish and had a slight accent. He told me he was."

Holly opened a folder, looked over the pages inside. There was a photo of Delgado taken shortly before his death that was found in the house where he was killed and another when he was a young boy, about 14. In both, he had jet-black hair, and his skin was a dark tan. Holly looked up at her client.

"He was actually the product of a white father and a black mother," she said. "The mother's parents were not excited about having a mixed race grandchild and forced her to put the baby up for adoption."

Holly pushed the folder across the bare metal table to Bonnie. She shuffled through the material inside and found a photo of a couple that matched Holly's description.

"But he knew Spanish and he talked to me about visiting family in Mexico," Bonnie said, thoroughly puzzled.

"He was adopted by a Mexican couple here in Wyoming," Holly explained. "They did not speak much English, although being here illegally, they tried to learn. So, your former husband learned enough Spanish to get by."

She paused a moment to let that sink in, and to allow Bonnie to read the adoption papers that were in the folder.

"Surely you wondered why a Latino man had a first name that was more Caucasian than Latino," Holly said.

"I never thought about it," Bonnie said very monotone.

Holly thought about that a moment. Considering the trauma she went through with her first husband's death and the aftermath, it did make sense that Bonnie didn't give much thought into her actions and decisions at the time. She had a small boy to support and could not do it on her own.

"His stories about Mexico and visiting family were probably true, since his adoptive parents were from Sinaloa," Holly said.

Bonnie was dumbstruck. How could she have been so misled?

But several weeks later, Holly was back with even more information about Bonnie's victim. This time it had a bearing on her case.

When Holly walked into the ten-foot by ten-foot interview room with the table and two metal chairs, Bonnie had no reaction from where she sat to the broad smile on her attorney's face.

"I have some more information about Delgado and it's not about his family history," she said as she sat in the chair opposite Bonnie.

Holly had avoided using Delgado's name as much as possible, as she could tell Bonnie was very uncomfortable whenever it came up. But she was growing tired of thinking up new descriptions for him. Besides, Bonnie would be hearing the name a lot as the legal process moved forward, and she decided her client needed to get used to hearing it – a lot.

The look on Bonnie's face changed very little. She had been very quiet in the visits Holly had with her since Delgado's family history was revealed. She was still stewing over being so easily deceived by him, in addition to the abuse.

"You told me he was a truck driver," Holly said. "Did he ever talk about what he was hauling?"

Bonnie shook her head but said nothing.

"Well, he had a couple of different cargos," Holly said. "One was drugs from the Sinaloa cartel and the other was illegal immigrants."

After what she had heard about him earlier, Bonnie was not surprised by this revelation.

"What does that have to do with my case?" Bonnie asked, for the first time showing a slight interest in the charges leveled at her.

"It really has nothing to do with what happened in that house to Delgado," Holly said, and continued before Bonnie could chime in. "But it is going to affect you personally."

"How is that?" Bonnie asked.

"The Drug Enforcement Agency has been building a case against the Sinaloa cartel and its operations in the U.S.," Holly explained. "They had Delgado in their sights, hoping to either turn him against the cartel or prosecute him for his involvement."

She paused to let Bonnie take that information in and process it. She was also hoping Bonnie would say something that would move the conversation along. Holly was worried about her client's apparent disinterest in her own case – or maybe it was all too overwhelming. Holly believed it was the former.

"They will want to interrogate you," Holly said a little forcefully. "They'll want to know if you were involved in his activities."

"I wasn't involved in that. I didn't even know about it until you told me," Bonnie said with no emotion in her voice.

"You were married to the man. How could you not know what he was into?" Holly asked, both for her own curiosity and to test how Bonnie would react.

"He never told me anything except that he was a truck driver," Bonnie responded in the same flat tone.

"But weren't you ever curious about it? You never asked him?" the lawyer asked, again for the same reasons.

"He was so mean to me I was fine not talking to him," was Bonnie's response.

"You put up with that for two years. There must have been something about it you liked," Holly said. "I would have left his ass long ago."

Since she had driven the knife into Delgado's chest, Bonnie's eyes took on a different color. They became battleship gray, showing the detachment with life she was developing because she had decided to take the fall for her second husband's death to try and hide her son's involvement. But when Holly chastised her for staying with Delgado, the algae color began to return.

"Do you have children, Ms. Quarters?" Bonnie asked.

The lawyer shook her head.

"Then you haven't got a clue what it's like to try and raise a child on your own," Bonnie said.

Holly noticed the change in Bonnie's eye color and the firm tone that was now part of her speech pattern. She was pleased. That meant there was some fight in Bonnie, after all.

"No, I don't," Holly said. "But there were resources that would have helped you," she added, hoping it would provoke Bonnie more.

"But you do know what it's like to have a controlling abuser have power over you," she said, her eyes going from algae colored to the light green, and her voice becoming sterner.

"Yes, that is true, to an extent," Holly replied. "But I had the courage to take steps to make it stop and punish the guy."

Bonnie's eyes then went neon green, and she jumped up from her chair and pounded the table.

"Well, good for you," she hollered. "I wasn't as strong as you. I believed I had no options. So, because I was a gutless bitch, you think I deserve to rot in prison."

Though Bonnie's sudden outburst had taken her by surprise, Holly did not react physically. But inside, she was all but jumping for joy. She had finally broken through Bonnie's shell of indifference to her fate and sparked some fire in her. It was the last ingredient she needed to complete a defense for her. The fact that Bonnie's anger was directed at her own attorney at the moment was of little consequence. Redirecting it would be an easy task for Holly.

But there was still a lot of other work to do.

Chapter 6

Lauralei was tired of fielding the same question from Curtis day in and day out.

"When is Mom coming home?"

Her only answer was to tell her friend's son that she did not know. While she was tired of hearing the question repeated seemingly without end, her sympathy for the boy grew each time he asked it.

Lauralei had, with Bonnie's permission, explained to Curtis exactly where his mother was and why she was there. And as agonizing as it was to hear his queries about when she was going to come home, it was even more so to hear him insist, on a daily basis, that it was he, not his mother, who had plunged the knife into Delgado four times.

Try as she might, Lauralei could not picture Curtis doing such a thing. He was a quiet, well-mannered young boy, despite all the drunkenness and violence he had seen from his stepfather over the past two years. Because of that experience, he shied away from even the hint of confrontation.

In addition, though he was a bit big for his tender age of seven, Curtis had never shown any indication he had the strength to plunge a large butcher knife into a person four times, burying the entire blade into the body on three of the four wounds.

But he was very insistent that it was he, and he alone, who had ended Delgado's life.

His description of that fateful night never altered. When he was questioned by Albany County detectives, he claimed Delgado was again beating on his mother. She ran into Curtis' room, but before she could shut and lock the door, he was inside. While he was slapping and punching his mother, Curtis skirted out of the room, ran to the kitchen, grabbed the biggest knife he could find and returned to his room.

Once there, he found Delgado lying on his bed on his left side, his hands around his mother's throat. Curtis claimed he brought the knife down as hard as he could on his stepfather's right side. Screaming like a little girl who saw a spider, he rolled off the bed onto his back on the floor. Curtis claimed he jumped on Delgado's sizable paunch and, using both hands, drove the knife into his body three more times.

He even included the fact that he stomped on Delgado's crotch.

The detectives had him repeat the description several times, asking different questions each time to try and throw him off. But Curtis told the same story each and every time.

The cops even suggested it was his mother who actually handled the knife during the deed.

"No, it was me," Curtis said each time it was suggested his mother was the actual killer.

He told the same story to Lauralei and pleaded with her to tell the police so his mother could come home. She complied once.

"His mother is telling a completely different story," McWeeny had told her. "We're inclined to believe her."

He added the only part of Curtis' story that seemed to have any truth to it was him stomping on Delgado's crotch. The autopsy showed considerable bruising on his penis and testicles. But by the time those blows were delivered, the doctor who did the post-mortem exam was certain the man had succumbed to the stab wounds and had not felt anything from what was believed to be Curtis' first and last attack upon his stepfather.

"But I even find it a little far-fetched that the boy did that," McWeeny told Lauralei. "There was no indication of that kind of violence from the boy during his short life."

The plan Bonnie had worked out with Lauralei was to make life as normal as possible for Curtis. In that vein, he had only missed one day of school – the day after Delgado was killed.

But the boy made a normal-as-possible life difficult because all he could think about was the incident at home and the fact his mother was in jail. In small towns, word spreads fast – and in most cases, whatever story is going around gets embellished with each telling. So, by the time he returned to school, everyone there knew what had happened and who was involved.

Albany had no schools, so youngsters who lived there were bussed twenty minutes to Centennial for their schooling. It was a larger town, but the same rules of gossip applied, only amplified.

The word spread among the school's adult staff, and what they lacked in actual details of the incident, they filled in the gaps with their imaginations. No matter how much the adults tried to keep the talk amongst themselves – and they didn't try very hard – the young students heard some snatches of conversations and let their own imaginations build a story. No two versions were exactly the same.

While Curtis had been an enthusiastic and outgoing child in his first few years, he lost some of that as he watched his mother go through the grief of losing her husband. Through the brutal years with Delgado, he began to turn more inward. After the killing, some anger started to creep into his personality.

During those bus rides to school and throughout his days in the building, he heard the whispers behind his back. He also noticed the other children his age and a year or two older keeping their distance from him, including the friends he had made. He was feeling isolated, and he was resenting it. That added to the anger that was building in him.

Bonnie sat quietly at the defense table next to Holly. It was her arraignment, and Holly had briefed her thoroughly before the proceedings.

"This is going to be a formality," Holly had said. "There is plenty of evidence to take this to trial. But I don't want you to be concerned about that."

"Why not?" Bonnie asked, a little sternly, but she had come to trust Holly.

"Because I believe I have enough evidence to show this was a justified killing," she answered.

"If that's the case, why not present that evidence in the arraignment and that would be the end of it?" Bonnie asked.

"Because this is only a hearing to determine whether there is enough evidence to have a trial, not the time for me to present all of my evidence," Holly said. "If I do that in this proceeding, the prosecution will know in advance our planned defense."

Bonnie had watched enough crime TV shows to have a different idea of how court proceedings worked.

"But isn't there something called discovery, where you have to give that to them anyway before the trial?" she asked.

Holly always got frustrated when clients brought up the discovery process. She knew where they were learning about how the court system worked. What none of them understood was that Hollywood took shortcuts to advance the stories they were telling.

"You are correct about the discovery," Holly said. "But it's not like it is on TV. We are obligated to share our evidence and witnesses, but there is no timeline that specifies when that has to take place. The prosecution does have to share with us everything they have."

Bonnie was skeptical, but trusted in what Holly had to say.

"And there are cases where the matter is settled before trial, and most of the time, in those instances, that happens before the defense shares anything," Holly added.

"Do you think that might happen in my case?" Bonnie asked.

Holly did have an idea that Bonnie's case could settle before trial. But she did not share that with her client.

"Anything is possible," is all she said.

Holly had been right about the arraignment being a formality. The judge made sure Bonnie had an attorney and provided her with information about her rights under the law. She was then asked how she wanted to plead.

"Not guilty, your honor," she said, following Holly's instructions to the letter.

As expected, the arraignment judge found there was enough evidence to send the case to trial. It was set to start in sixty days.

"That gives me enough time to go over what the prosecution has and research some other avenues," Holly told Bonnie at the end of the proceedings. "I'll be talking to you regularly. I'll want to get some more information from you about the killing and the years leading up to it."

"I'll tell you whatever you need," Bonnie said.

Holly wanted to keep the fighting spirit in Bonnie that she had drawn out. She also wanted to let her know that she had a lot to look forward to when this was all over.

"Remember, you have a son to raise, and you can't do it from prison," she said. "I'm going to do everything I can to make sure he has his mother to raise him."

Because she was being charged with murder and the judge agreed with the prosecution that she was a fight risk, Bonnie was not released on her own recognizance. Her bail was also set so high there was no way she could come up with the cash to get out of jail; even going through a bail bondsman was not enough.

The prosecutor and Holly met, as required by the court, shortly after the arraignment to discuss a possible plea agreement. This could have reduced the time Bonnie would spend in prison.

But in an odd twist, the prosecutor offered no plea deal. He was determined to seek a guilty plea or conviction at trial. He was very confident the physical evidence gave him an iron-clad conviction.

That stance saved Holly the trouble of arguing with the prosecutor. She had no intention of accepting any deal that meant her client had to spend any more time in jail than she already was. She was certain she could get Bonnie acquitted by making a case of self-defense and the protection of her son.

When she explained all this to Bonnie, she got no objections from her client. With her rediscovered gumption, thanks to Holly pressing her so hard, she was ready to fight the prosecution as well.

Bonnie's pretrial hearing was scheduled ten days after the arraignment. Holly visited her every day, going over the details of that fateful night in her home each day. She wanted to make sure Bonnie's telling of the events remained the same each time. She was ready to coach her where needed. But that turned out to be unnecessary where the events of that night were concerned. Bonnie's retellings never waivered. Holly only provided advice on her appearance in court and her demeaner.

Holly did caution her client about the drug and human trafficking aspects of Delgado's life.

"Because of that, the DEA is going to want to talk to you," she said. "They're going to want to know what you knew about your husband's activities."

"But I didn't know anything about that," Bonnie said.

"They're not going to believe that," Holly told her. "They'll take the approach that you were his wife and you must have known something."

"So, what do I say to them?" Bonnie asked.

This was something Holly did not want Bonnie to have to deal with alone. She knew that government agents could be very intimidating with frightened people already in dire straights with the legal system.

"There is only one word I want you to say to every question they ask you," Holly said. "Lawyer."

The puzzled look on Bonnie's face told Holly she needed to explain.

"When you were arrested, the officers did read you your Miranda rights, correct?" she asked. When Bonnie nodded her head, she went on. "Those rights give you the option of talking to law enforcement, but it also gives you the right to have an attorney present while you are being questioned."

"But I've already talked to the deputies and told them everything that happened that night," Bonnie said.

"That doesn't matter; you can invoke a lawyer at any time, even after you've provided some or all the details," Holly explained. "Besides, what the DEA is going to want to know is different from the killing of your husband."

"And all I have to say is lawyer, and they'll have to stop asking me things?" Bonnie asked.

"They will continue to try to get you to talk, but just remember to answer every question with that one word – lawyer," Holly said.

Chapter 7

It didn't take the DEA long to pay their visit to Bonnie. They had her in the interview room in the county jail complex the very next day.

Bonnie sat across the table in her orange jumpsuit with her hands secured in cuffs connected by a chain running through a large steel handcuff ring bolted to the tabletop. Across from her were two DEA agents who could have been twins. Both had dark brown hair and blue eyes. Their faces were pretty plain, unlike the chiseled faces seen in movies and TV shows. It was clear they both worked out some, but not obsessively. To Bonnie, they could have passed as computer nerds.

"We want to know what your former husband was into," Neil Cole said.

Bonnie didn't move, didn't even flinch. She stared straight ahead, only occasionally averting her eyes from one agent to the other.

"Your former husband, Logan Delgado," Raymond Peck said, leaning slightly forward, as if Bonnie was hard of hearing and getting closer would help.

Her stoic stare continued. The agents looked at each other, giving the unspoken signal that it was time to employ a different tactic.

"What was your involvement in your husband's activities?" Peck asked.

"Lawyer," Bonnie said firmly.

That response took them a little by surprise. It took them a moment to recover. But when they did, they continued their questioning.

"How were you involved in his smuggling of illegal drugs?" Cole asked.

If her attorney had not clued her in, this question would have taken Bonnie completely by surprise. While Delgado's abuse had kept her from even wanting to ask about his activities outside of work or their home, she also had trouble envisioning a drunk like her second husband having the wherewithal to be involved in anything that would require a sharp mind.

"Lawyer," Bonnie said with a little more volume in her voice.

She noticed a look of frustration spread across both agents' faces. Their muscles also tensed up. They had walked into the interview room knowing Bonnie's background – the death of her first husband, the abuse from her second, the fact she had a young son. They assumed they would be dealing with a broken woman who would be easily intimidated into providing the information they needed to help build their case. And that's exactly what they would have found if Holly Quarters hadn't entered her life and sparked a fire in her belly.

"Look, Ms. Delgado, we…." Peck began, but was cut off.

"Herden," Bonnie said.

Cole opened the folder in front of him and read the name under the photo. He looked up at Bonnie then down at the photo again, as if the name would magically match what Bonnie was saying.

"It says here you are, Bonnie Delgado," he said without raising his head.

"Herden," Bonnie repeated.

The agents exchanged a look and shrugged.

"We know, Ms. Herden, or whatever you are calling yourself, that your husband was involved in smuggling drugs and illegal aliens," Cole said, with sarcasm dripping off the six words following her name. "As his wife, you must have known what he was up to."

"Lawyer," Bonnie said, adding another octave to her voice.

"Ms. Herden, you are facing charges of murder," Peck said. "You don't want to add obstruction of justice to the charges."

"Lawyer," Bonnie hollered, changing the agent's looks from frustration to anger.

"You're going to help us or we can make sure you never see your son again," Cole blurted out.

"Lawyer!" Bonnie screamed.

The interview room they were in did not have a two-way mirror with officers watching from the other side. But Bonnie's last call for a lawyer was so loud it was heard faintly by the deputy standing guard on the other side of the door. The room was built to be somewhat soundproof, but if the sounds inside were loud enough, they could be heard outside by someone standing close enough to the door.

The deputy opened the door and looked in. The DEA agents turned and gave him sour looks. Cole was about to protest the interruption, but Bonnie beat him to the punch.

"I want my lawyer," she yelled.

With the door open, her voice carried to the area outside the room. Within seconds, Albany County Sheriff Jesse Moore was at the door. Bonnie repeated her request as soon as he appeared.

"OK, gentlemen, the interview is over; she has invoked her lawyer," the sheriff said.

The agents remained in their seats.

"We're federal agents, and we trump the invocation of lawyers," Peck said.

"Not in my jail you don't," Moore said, waggling his right index finger beckoning the agents to leave the room. "Let's go."

The agents, almost simultaneously, stood and walked to the door. Cole got nearly nose-to-nose with the sheriff.

"This isn't over," he snarled. "We'll get a court order."

Moore let a smile play at the corners of his mouth.

"Tell Judge Jackson I said hello," he said smugly.

Shortly after getting the call from the school, Lauralei went to her boss at the grocery store where she worked as a cashier and asked to leave work early. She had explained to him when she took Curtis in that she might have to do this from time to time as long as the boy was in her charge.

When she had told Jim Warner then about her situation, he seemed accommodating.

"Anything you need," he had said.

But now, he seemed to change his mind.

"You know we're short-handed today," he said. "You're the only cashier we have today."

In the years she had worked at the store, there had been plenty of times employees were allowed to leave work early in difficult circumstances – even when the store was low on staff.

Just a couple of weeks ago, Jim had allowed another cashier to leave early and he took over her station for the rest of the day.

But now, he wasn't going to allow it when Lauralei made the request. She couldn't help but think it was because of the killing of Delgado. He knew Bonnie was in jail in connection with the incident, and he knew Bonnie and Lauralei were friends.

"But there's something wrong at Curtis' school, they want me to go there as soon as I can," she protested. "I'm responsible for the boy while his mother's unable to take care of him. " She couldn't bring herself to say that she was in jail.

"I understand that, but school will be out in a couple of hours, and I've already adjusted your daily work schedule to allow you to leave in time to get there for that, as we agreed. The boy can wait until then."

He turned and walked away, making sure Lauralei could not continue to press her case. For the next two hours, she did her job as best she could, sick with worry about Curtis and pissed off at Jim. She was sure customers could tell. But she did not care. When her shift finally ended, she hurriedly clocked out and headed for Centennial.

At the school, she went directly to the principal's office. The secretary was still there and showed her into the inner office.

"Hello, Lauralei, I'm glad you could come, though I was expecting you hours ago," said Blaine Martinelli, the school principal, who remained seated behind his desk. The irritated look on his face put Lauralei on the defensive.

"My boss wouldn't let me leave early," she shot back, still standing.

The revelation did nothing to change the expression on the principal's face. He did not ask her to sit down.

"Curtis was involved in a fight in his classroom," Martinelli said. "One boy ended up with some fairly serious injuries and a girl got a bump on the head when she was knocked over by the boy Curtis was pummeling."

Lauralei was not totally surprised. She knew about the harassment Curtis had been taking in the past few days. And she noticed his self-isolation and darkening moods.

"What happened in the classroom?" Lauralei asked.

"Everyone we have talked to – the teacher and students – tells pretty much the same story," Martinelli said. "Curtis suddenly lashed out at this boy for no reason."

While she was not surprised that Curtis may have lost his temper, she doubted he did so unprovokedly.

"He has been getting bullied lately. Maybe the boy was doing that," Lauralei said.

"That is not the facts we are getting from everyone else in that classroom," Martinelli said, getting a little defensive himself.

Lauralei had heard the gossip around Albany about Bonnie and Curtis. She had fielded some unsavory comments from a few people because they knew she and Bonnie were friends. She recognized that she was playing against a stacked deck and further attempts to defend Curtis would fall on deaf ears.

"Where is he? I'll take him home," she said.

"First, I need to let you know what we are going to do going forward," Martinelli said. "We don't want to deprive Curtis of his education. But we can't put him back into the classroom where he could hurt someone even worse."

The hair on the back of Lauralei's neck stood straight up. There was something coming that was not going to set well with her, or Curtis' mother.

"He'll be put in a class at the Education Service District where he will be taught one-on-one by one of their specialists," Martinelli said.

Lauralei clinched her fists and could feel the heat in her cheeks. She was sure Martinelli could see her anger rising because he stood up and appeared to be girding himself for a tongue-lashing. He was relieved when it didn't come.

"Just tell me where he is, and I'll get him out of here," she said.

"I'll have him brought here," Martinelli said and left the office to speak to his secretary.

When Curtis walked into the office, Lauralei saw no fear in the boy. Instead, he had a very stern look on his face. He remained silent through the entire drive back to Albany. So did Lauralei. She knew the ESD office was in Laramie, which meant there would be no bus rides. She would have to take him and pick him up there. That meant trying to make a new arrangement with her boss. Considering their earlier exchange, that was not going to go over well.

Bonnie was devastated when Holly told her about Curtis' move to the ESD in Laramie. She knew the extra burden this would place on her friend she had tasked with taking care of her son. But more importantly, she was extremely concerned for Curtis' state of mind. Even before she was sent to jail, Bonnie saw that her son's character and attitude were changing since his father died. Added to that was the abuse and violence he witnessed through his mother's marriage to Delgado, followed by his death and their involvement in it. She saw he was becoming more withdrawn and angry as the days went on.

Now, she was in jail and unable to care for him, and she had refused to allow him to visit her while she was incarcerated.

She also knew about the bullying he was enduring. And because of that, he had been taken from his school environment. She was certain that would add to his anger and frustration.

"Would it be possible for him to visit me?" she asked Holly after she explained the current situation. "And why didn't Lauralei come here herself to tell me all this?"

"Lauralei is busy trying to get a new job," Holly explained. "She tried to work out a different schedule at the store so she could drive Curtis to the ESD in Laramie, but her boss fired her instead."

Bonnie was horrified that her friend lost her job because she was trying to help her out with Curtis. She was speechless for a few moments, and Holly went on during her silence.

"I have some friends at a law firm in Laramie and I sent her over there for an interview," Holly said. "That way, she can take Curtis to the ESD when she goes over to work."

"Do you think she'll get the job?" Bonnie asked hopefully, not just for her friend but for Curtis as well.

"Lauralei is a sharp girl and seems to learn quickly. I spent some time talking with her before I sent her there," Holly said. "I think she has a pretty good chance on her own merits. But they also owe me some favors, so that couldn't hurt either."

That provided some measure of relief for Bonnie. Selfishly, she knew that if Lauralei stayed employed, Curtis would continue to be well cared for. But she was also relieved for Lauralei. She needed a steady income to keep her head above water. While she continued to see men, she was not going to depend on them for her emotional or financial needs.

"Fool me once, shame on you, fool me twice, shame on me," she often told Bonnie when they talked about their chances of getting involved in a committed relationship with men.

"Now we need to talk about you," Holly interrupted Bonnie's train of thought.

"I don't think the DEA is convinced you knew nothing about Delgado's activities in the drug and human smuggling trade," she said.

"But I didn't know anything about it," Bonnie interjected before her attorney could get another word out.

"I believe you," Holly said. "But they don't, so expect more from them."

Holly opened a folder sitting in front of her and flipped through some pages in silence for a few seconds. Bonnie watched her with some expectation, but not a lot of enthusiasm. Her thoughts kept going back to Curtis and what he must be going through.

"My long-term goal in this is to argue that you are not guilty because you were protecting yourself and your son," Holly explained. "It is called 'Stand Your Ground.' Do you know what this is?"

"Vaguely. It says a person can kill someone if they think they could be hurt badly or killed," Bonnie said.

"It is a little more complicated than that, but essentially that's it," Holly said.

She took a moment to read a few of the pages in her folder before continuing.

"I'll make the argument that not only were you in fear of serious bodily injury or death for yourself, but for Curtis as well," Holly explained.

"And that will get me out of jail?" Bonnie asked.

"The prosecution will argue that the law only applies if there is an intruder who is threatening you, and since your husband lived there, he wasn't an intruder," Holly said. She saw Bonnie's spark of enthusiasm fizzle. She went on to try and keep her client upbeat.

"The law does allow for some interpretation on that point," Holly said. "The prosecutors will also argue that because you went to the kitchen, you had an opportunity to escape the situation…"

"But I wasn't going to leave Curtis there with him," Bonnie interrupted angrily. "No telling what that asshole would have done to him."

"Yes, I know," Holly said soothingly. "And that will be my argument. You stayed to protect your son."

"Do you think that will be enough?" Bonnie asked, calmer this time.

Holly paused for a moment before answering. She was treading on thin ice with that question.

"I can't make any promises, Bonnie, because a lot will depend on the jury that is selected," Holly explained. "It also depends on how much leeway the judge will give me."

"What does that mean, leeway?" Bonnie asked.

"There are certain rules about what can be presented to the jury and what can't," Holly said. "I want to get it in the jury's mind about Delgado's criminal activity. But since that does not directly relate to his death and how it came about, it might not be allowed."

Again, Bonnie's initial excitement faded from her expression.

"I could bring it up in court, and the judge could instruct the jury to ignore it in their deliberations," Holly said.

"And they have to ignore it?" Bonnie asked.

"Yes, that is the theory," Holly said. "But when something like that is said, even if the judge throws it out and tells the jury that they can't use that information to make their decision, it will still be in their minds. It will have an effect, whether they know it or not."

At that moment, Holly's cell phone pinged. She opened the incoming text and read it, a smile playing at the corners of her mouth.

"That was Lauralei," she told Bonnie. "She got the job in Laramie – at twice what she was making at the store."

As the words settled into her brain, Bonnie broke down and cried.

Chapter 8

Dean Pasaat sat in the waiting area outside the Wyoming governor's office in the sprawling building on Capitol Avenue in Cheyenne. Originally built before Wyoming was a state, the initial structure was three-stories but small compared to its current building, a Renaissance Revival reminiscent of the United States Capitol in Washington, D.C. It included a copper dome that, over the years, tarnished so much that state officials covered it in gold leaf. Wing extensions on the east and west sides of the building were added over the years.

Pasaat, who was busy overseeing preparations for a pre-trial hearing for the Delgado killing in his county, was called the previous day by Governor Clark Hardon's chief of staff and told the governor wanted to meet with him. Pasaat did not know exactly what the meeting was to be about, but he did have an idea.

While not the only murder in Albany County, the Delgado killing had garnered a great deal of attention. Most of that was because of the circumstances – an abusive man threatening his wife, who then protected herself and her young son with, using the courtroom parlance, extreme prejudice. But the undercurrent of attention for the case came from his other activities.

In Wyoming, the county prosecuting attorney have the responsibilities of a district attorney. It is an elected position, and Pasaat would be facing re-election if he wanted to stay in office. And he did.

"You may go in now," the governor's secretary said from her station behind her plain wooden desk. She did not get up to open the door to the governor's office, but returned to her laptop keyboard where there was a long list of tasks to perform in the next two hours before she went home to her husband and children.

When Pasaat entered the governor's large, ornate office, Governor Hardon stood up behind his oak desk with its grandiose carvings along the edges and down the corners. The governor came forward with an extended hand. Pasaat took the hand and gave the governor a firm handshake, which was returned in kind.

"Please, have a seat," the governor said, gesturing toward a brown leather sofa. Pasaat sat at one end, and the governor chose a Victorian chair directly across from the prosecuting attorney.

While the prosecutor and governor had met before, they did not know each other well. What Pasaat did know was that the governor was an avid fisherman. He had been throughout the state on fishing trips during his time off and whenever he had business in the towns around the sparsely populated state. He also knew about his favorite fishing spots.

"You been up to Dubois lately?" Pasaat asked.

The town of around 600 people sandwiched between the Absaroka and Wind River mountain ranges about 70 miles southeast of the southern entrance to Yellowstone National Park was considered one of Wyoming's typical Old West towns. Horse Creek, originating high in the Absaroka Mountains north of the town, emptied into the Wind River that skirted the town's southern side at the foot of the Wind River Mountains. Both were thriving with rainbow and brown trout.

"Not in a couple of months," Hardon said. "It's been too long. Do you ever get up there?"

Pasaat, who grew up in Ohio, was not much of an outdoorsman and didn't get out to the rural areas much in the ten years he had lived in Wyoming.

"No, I've never been up there," he replied. "I have thought about going to Yellowstone, just haven't had the time."

"Well, you should make the time," Hardon said. "It's beautiful up there. Maybe next time I go, I'll invite you along."

"Maybe I can work it out," Pasaat replied, but he knew the chances were slim that it would come to pass.

Both men fell silent through an awkward pause. It was the governor who spoke first.

"You've got yourself quite a case over there in Albany County," he said. "That woman who stabbed her husband," he offered in response to Pasaat's puzzled expression.

"Oh, yeah, that one," Pasaat finally said. "But it seems pretty much a sure thing. She confessed to killing him. I'm just hoping the defender will go for a plea deal."

Hardon tapped the eraser end of a pencil he was holding on the arm of the chair a few times before he spoke again.

"I know Holly Quarters' reputation," Hardon said. "She's like a dog with a bone when she has a case that she believes in. You can forget about a plea agreement on this one."

Pasaat also knew Holly's reputation. But since Bonnie had relayed the details of what happened in the house that fateful night and did not try to hide her involvement in her husband's death, he believed Holly's chances of getting her client acquitted were slim.

"It might not be easy, but I'm sure she'll see that she can't win this one," he told the governor.

Hardon stood up and tossed the pencil onto the top of his desk. It rolled toward the edge and dropped off into his plush office chair. The governor took a few paces around the desk and then turned to face Pasaat, who remained seated on the sofa.

"You and I are both facing an election," the governor said. "This case, if it goes to trial, could seriously hurt both our chances of getting re-elected."

Pasaat was a little puzzled. How could a slam dunk murder case be detrimental to his re-election? And more puzzling, how could it affect the governor's chances of staying in office?

He had been appointed by Hardon to the office just over a year ago after the sitting prosecutor was killed in a violent late-night multi-vehicle pileup on Highway 487 during one of Wyoming's sudden blizzards. He had been in the state's largest city to watch his grandson play basketball in a regional high school tournament. Pasaat had left a thriving private practice to take the job, so he wanted to remain in office.

"How can this one case keep us from winning an election?" he asked.

Hardon shook his head and, picking up the pencil that had rolled onto his chair, sat down in the high-back office seat behind his desk. He did not realize how politically naïve the man sitting across from him really was.

"This is not the Wyoming of the '60s and '70s when men dominated over women and men could beat their wives with impunity," he explained. "That kind of thinking is looked down upon now. If a man beats on a woman, or vice versa, now there has to be consequences."

"I'm aware, governor," Pasaat said a little testily. "But there have to be consequences for murder as well."

The governor sighed. He was going to have to paint a picture for the prosecutor.

"I agree," he said. "But the reality we face is that the word has already gotten around that the woman you are trying to prosecute was routinely abused by her husband."

He picked up a copy of the *Wyoming Tribune Eagle* from an end table and tossed it to Pasaat. He read the lead headline: "Abused Albany women on trial for murder." He read through the first few paragraphs, which detailed townspeople's quotes talking about Delgado's treatment of his wife.

"This is also in the *Casper Star Tribune,* and I'm sure it will be on K2, if it hasn't been already," Hardon said. "And this is the digital age. This is going to be all over social media."

Pasaat was about to argue again for Bonnie, facing the consequences of her actions, when the governor held up his index finger.

"And check out the sidebar story to that one," he said, and waited for Pasaat to find it and scan the headline. "Your victim was apparently deep into drug and human smuggling."

Again, Pasaat began to protest, this time that Delgado's guilt in those areas were not proven, when the governor's finger went up.

"When that starts getting around, along with his abuse of his wife, the voters are going to take more of an interest in this case. And if she is convicted, they're not going to be happy."

Hardon paused to see if Pasaat still wanted to protest. When he remained silent, the governor went on.

"On the other hand, if you look at this from the perspective her lawyer will present – that of an abused wife trying to protect herself and her young son – you will surely see the value of letting this one go," Hardon said. "And she got a piece of cow shit off your county's boot, and the state's."

Bonnie shuddered as she walked through the door of the home she had shared with Delgado. She was glad she had been able to re-enter the house without Curtis and Lauralei. She did not know how she would react and did not want her son and closest friend witnessing it if she lost it.

As her car and Delgado's truck were at the house, she had no way to get to the house on her own. So Holly offered to drive her there. She also offered to stay as long as Bonnie needed her. The lawyer stayed a couple of paces behind her client as she entered the house where she had stabbed her husband to death. Rather, she and Curtis had stabbed him to death. A few tears rolled down her cheeks when she reminded herself that Curtis had been involved.

She took a few hesitant steps past the front door and stopped to look around. Since the violence happened in Curtis' bedroom at the end of the hall directly in front of her, nothing was out of place in the kitchen and living room. She did glance into the kitchen and spied the knife block in the corner of the counter. The slot for the largest knife was empty. The police had offered to give it back to her when she was released less than an hour ago, but she refused to take it. She didn't want any reminders of what she had done.

She looked down the hallway and felt a little faint. She felt Holly's hands steady her by the shoulders.

"Are you alright?" the lawyer asked.

Bonnie stood there for a few moments, soaking in the comfort from her attorney's firm hold on her shoulders.

"Uh, yeah," she stammered. But Holly knew better. The lawyer steered Bonnie toward the sofa and sat her down, taking a seat next to her. She kept her left arm around her client's waist and grasped her hand with her right hand.

"This is going to take some time to adjust to," Holly said soothingly. "Are you sure you want to come back here so soon? I can arrange a motel for you for a week or so."

The county would not pay for it, Holly knew, but she was willing to do that for her client.

"No, I'll be alright," Bonnie said. "I need to have a stable home for Curtis."

Because Delgado had been so abusive to her during the past two years, she thought she would be so relieved that it was finally over that she would be okay with going back to live in the house. But her initial reactions when she came into the house gave her pause. She needed to see how deep her trepidation was.

Bonnie stood up, and Holly followed suit.

"I need to see the rest of the house," she said. "It needs to be ready for Curtis to come home."

She was trembling. Holly squeezed her hand.

"You don't need to do this," the lawyer offered. "We can find you a new place to live, and you can stay in a motel in the meantime."

Holly knew that was easier said than done. Rental homes were hard to come by despite the slowdown in oil and natural gas production in the area that had those renters who worked in the industry moving to other locales. The homes were snapped up quickly by students from the university in Laramie and tourists who wanted short-term rentals. Besides, with that kind of market, rents were higher than Bonnie could afford, even when she was employed, if that was even possible in the current emotional climate in the community.

"No, I need to get settled again, for Curtis," Bonnie said. She was also aware of the housing situation in the county.

She started down the hallway toward the bedroom doors at the far end. Halfway there, she saw the blood stains on the carpet where she had collapsed in terror after the stabbing. She felt faint again, and Holly squeezed her hand tighter.

But Bonnie hesitated only a moment to let the faintness pass. She walked to the end of the hallway and looked into the master bedroom. The sheet and covers on the bed were still as they had been that night. As she turned her head, she took in the bathroom straight ahead. She could still see blood in the sink from where Lauralei had washed her hands, a hand towel was on the floor with small brown stains from dried blood and vomit remnants were on the toilet seat from where Lauralei had puked.

Bonnie shivered, and Holly, still grasping one of Bonnie's hands, tried to pull her back down the hallway toward the living room. But Bonnie broke the lawyer's grip on her hand and moved into the doorway to Curtis' room. On the floor next to his bed was a large rust-colored stain where Delgado had bled out from the stab wounds until the paramedics came to attend to him.

Holly could see Bonnie's knees go wobbly and then she crumbled to the floor before the attorney could get there to catch her.

Chapter 9

The initial shock of being back in the house where she killed her husband was overwhelming for Bonnie at first. Holly stayed with her for several hours, working to calm her nerves as best she could.

There came a point when Bonnie was not totally comfortable but no longer terrified. She convinced Holly she was ready to be left alone in the house.

"Alright, but you have my number if you need anything," the lawyer said, making sure her business card, with her private cell phone number written on it, was taped to the refrigerator. She made sure Bonnie knew it was there.

"Are you going to have Lauralei come over and bring Curtis?" Holly asked.

Bonnie violently shook her head.

"I need to get this place cleaned up first," Bonnie answered. "And I think it would be best to bring him back slowly."

"I'm sure he wants to see and be with his mother," Holly said. "Try and get him here as soon as possible."

As soon as Holly was gone and Bonnie was alone in the house, she had a sudden rush of nausea. Instead of going down the hallway to the bathroom, she went to the kitchen and hung her head over the sink. She had a few dry heaves, but there was no bile to come out. She stood at the sink and breathed deeply over and over until the nausea passed.

Unwilling to go back to the bedroom end of the house, she busied herself washing the few dishes that had sat in the sink during her absence. She then picked up the smattering of clothing and odds and ends that were left out the last time she, Delgado and Curtis were in the house together. Though the police had been in the house several times directly after the killing conducting their investigation, everything was left as they found it.

Keeping busy kept her mind off the killing and the current situation. But when all the busy work in the living room and kitchen was done, she was left standing in the middle of the living room, trying desperately to think of something else to do. The only thing she could think of was getting started cleaning the hallway, bathroom and the two bedrooms.

But she couldn't bring herself to even look down the hallway. It was still mid-afternoon, too early to sleep. Not that she could have anyway. She was too keyed up. Nor was she going to eat. She was not hungry, and she was afraid if she put anything in her stomach, it would just come right back up because she was so tense.

So she sat on the sofa and stared straight ahead for about thirty minutes. But now, sitting doing nothing to keep her mind occupied, she was replaying the events of the last few weeks, and that was not the road she wanted to travel. She picked up the remote and surfed through the television channels until she settled on reruns of situation comedies.

But before another thirty minutes could pass, she dropped off into a deep sleep. She was jolted awake by loud knocking at the front door. She sat up on the couch and realized she was sweating, her clothes drenched. While she could not remember the details, she knew she had been having nightmares. Bonnie was unaware of how long she had slept, but it must have been hours because no light bled in through the thin curtains that covered the large picture window across from the sofa.

Another, more insistent, knock at the door brought her out of her thoughts. When she opened it, Doris Gladstone, her landlady, stood on the small porch.

"Hello, Bonnie, how are you doing?" she asked, her empathy was only half-hearted.

"Uh, I'm adjusting," was all she could manage. She did not invite the woman inside.

"I wanted to talk to you about what you plan to do," Doris said in a business-like tome. When Bonnie could only muster a blank look, she continued. "Do you plan to stay in the house?"

"I guess so," Bonnie stammered, with the images of the blood stains in the hallway, bathroom and Curtis' bedroom flashing through her mind. She moved to the side and closed the door a little, hoping to hide the stains from the landlady.

Doris, a woman in her late-sixties with arthritic knees, shifted from one foot to the other, trying to hint that she should be invited inside so she could sit down. When Bonnie offered no such invitation, Doris huffed.

"Well, then I expect any mess that was made with that nasty business with your husband to be cleaned up right quick," the landlady instructed, turning to leave, and adding as she stepped off the porch, "And I expect the rent to be paid on time."

Bonnie stood in the half-open doorway and watched Doris walk along the narrow concrete path that led to the street, then get in her 1980 Chevy pickup that looked like it was held together by rust and drive away.

Bonnie was pretty sure she could handle getting the aftermath of the killing cleaned up, but she wasn't sure how she was going to afford the rent. There was no telling whether the waitress job she continued to work through her marriage to Delgado would still be available to her. If it was not, she would have to find something else. Delgado, even though he made plenty of money from his trucking job and sources Bonnie was only now starting to find out about, had insisted she turn over half her earnings to him, claiming it was her obligation to provide her fair share for the household expenses.

She had been able to save some of what she had left, but in two years, it hadn't amounted to enough to cover all the expenses she would have until she could get another job if the restaurant owner wouldn't take her back.

She finally shut the door, went back to the sofa and cried until she fell asleep again, returning to the nightmares.

Curtis continued to be a problem, but it had been nothing violent since he went to the ESD. During the drives back and forth with Lauralei, he was silent the entire time, no matter how much she tried to engage him in conversation. He was self-isolating.

It was no different in the classroom. There were five students being taught there, rather than the one-on-one situation Martinelli had told Lauralei would be the case. The other four were interactive with the teacher, to differing degrees. But Curtis was silent throughout the day while in the classroom. He also did not respond to the other children during breaks in the school day.

"Curtis is a bright boy, and knowledgeable with the coursework," Daniel Westberg, his ESD teacher, told Lauralei during a conference. "In quizzes and tests, he scores quite well. Higher than the other students, in fact."

He handed several sheets of paper – the last few quizzes and tests Curtis completed – over for her to examine. Lauralei was a little surprised. Knowing what Curtis had been through in the last two years, she imagined he would have difficulty concentrating enough to retain what was being taught.

"Is this normal for kids who are so withdrawn?" she asked. She wanted to get as much information as she could to provide to Curtis' mother.

"Not really," Daniel said. "In cases like these, we usually see scores go down, and in most cases, there is some acting out."

"Has he been acting out?" Lauralei asked, remembering the incident at the school that got him sent to ESD.

"Not at all," Daniel said. "I got a report from his school about the incident there and his records. There is no history of that for Curtis since he's been in school, except that one incident in Centennial. And there have been no problems here."

"He has been through a lot in the last couple of years, but there hasn't been anything like what happened at the school,"

Lauralei explained. "At least not that I've seen. And his mother has never mentioned anything like it."

Daniel sighed heavily and paused for a few moments. He was inwardly debating whether he should share what he was thinking with Lauralei, who was not the boy's mother. He avoided sharing too much of his own thoughts about a child with temporary guardians – and there were more of those than people would think.

But he was aware of the situation with Curtis' mother. It appeared Lauralei might be more than a temporary guardian.

"I'm going to tell you something that I don't normally share with anyone other than parents or legal guardians," Daniel said. "But considering the circumstances, I think I want you to know what I'm thinking."

Lauralei leaned forward in her chair, expecting to hear something terrible.

"In a lot of situations like these, when students show violent tendencies, even when it is only one instance, teachers don't want to have to deal with it and they pawn them off to someone else," Daniel said.

Lauralei's attentive expression turned to one of anger. Daniel realized he may not have chosen the best verbiage.

"That may sound harsh, but I can't blame the teachers," he offered. "They are under a lot of pressure, what with class sizes larger than they should be, they are working longer hours and with the prevailing entitlement attitude in society these days, they have a lot on their plates."

"But to just toss kids away like that, and especially Curtis who lost his father, had his stepfather die, and his mother goes to jail," Lauralei said. "Not that losing the stepfather was any big loss," she added.

Daniel cocked his head, like a dog when it sees something unusual.

"Oh, he beat Curtis' mom a lot, and he was about to do it to Curtis when…." Lauralei said, but stopped short, her hand shooting up to cover her mouth.

"This is the boy whose mother was arrested for killing that guy Logan Delgado," Daniel said, rubbing his chin and nodding slowly.

"That shouldn't mean Curtis should be punished," Lauralei blurted out defensively.

Daniel reached out and put his hand on Lauralei's.

"Trust me, I agree with you completely," he said. "And that's not going to happen here."

Lauralei felt reassured, but she wasn't ready to trust anyone completely. Bonnie had entrusted her to take care of Curtis, and she was determined to protect him as best she could. But so much was out of her hands.

"I'll work with Curtis one-on-one whenever I can to try and bring him out of his shell," Daniel said. "But keep in mind that my time is limited and I can't give the other students any less of my attention in the classroom setting."

Lauralei said she understood.

Curtis barely waited for Lauralei's car to come to a full stop at the curb outside the home he and his mother had shared with Delgado. The horror of that fateful, violent night did not enter his mind as he raced up the concrete sidewalk with weeds poking up from the joints and small cracks. He bounded up the three steps in one leap to the porch where his mother waited, threw his arms around her waist and buried his face into her belly.

It was the first time he had seen his mother since the night of the killing. He had missed her terribly. He had many questions about her absence, but those could wait until later. All he wanted now was to feel her body close to his and her loving embrace around him. For the first time in weeks, he felt safe and content.

In the forty-eight hours before that day, Lauralei and Bonnie had worked through the nights to clean the blood from the house as best they could. Their efforts gained only modest results, so the second day they called in professional cleaners. At the end of that day, anyone who had not seen the aftermath of Delgado's death would never have guessed there was a bloodletting in that house.

But Bonnie and Lauralei knew. They had seen it first hand and fresh. It was a sight that would be burned into their memories for the rest of their lives.

For Bonnie, though, she could find a way to live with the memory. Her biggest concern was whether Curtis remembered it as vividly – or at all. She had read that some young children who witness horrific events block the memory from their consciousness. If he did remember that night's events, to any degree, how would he react to being back in the house where they took place?

She had considered not going back to that house. But her financial situation was such that she could not afford a deposit and two-months rent to get into a new home. And the reality was that very little was available anyway. Even if she could somehow get into another house or apartment, how could she pay the month-to-month rent with no job?

Lauralei solved that problem. She offered to give notice at her apartment and move into the home with Bonnie and Curtis. She would pay the rent in full and pay all household expenses until Bonnie could get a job and contribute. Bonnie did not want to impose upon her friend.

"Besides, you have a job in Laramie now; you should find someplace to live there so you're not driving back and forth," Bonnie said.

"I don't need to live there," Lauralei said. "It's not too far to commute. And the cost of living is higher there."

Living in Bonnie's house offered lower rent than she would pay anywhere in Laramie, even in the shabbiest of places. It was a university town and landlords took full advantage of that.

"This works for me, because I'm also paying more at my apartment than here; and it works for you, because you and Curtis need a place to live," Lauralei said.

Bonnie was reluctant and offered other arguments against it. But they were half-hearted arguments, because she could see the logic in her friend's reasoning.

The only unknown yet to be determined was how Curtis would handle the situation. With some trepidation, the two women ushered him into the house, still clinging to his mother's waist.

Once inside, he tentatively looked around the living room and open kitchen. He seemed anxious and appeared to be looking for something – or someone. Apparently satisfied that Delgado was not in either room, he loosened his grip on his mother's midsection and took her hand in his. He looked up at her with a questioning look.

"It's okay, go ahead," she whispered.

She felt his hand slip from hers and he took a few tentative steps toward the hallway. He stopped and looked back at his mother, then Lauralei. They both nodded. Curtis turned back to the hallway and slowly walked to the end. He turned his head to the left and examined the master bedroom. He saw that his bed was now in there. He also saw that there was no one inside.

He turned his head forward and looked through the open door of the bathroom. It was also devoid of any person.

Curtis slowly turned his head to the right. His body tensed, as if he expected to see something – or someone – in there. But what he saw was the master bed was in what had been his room. He also saw his small dresser and toy box crammed in the corner and his mother's dresser in the open closet. Some of her clothing was also hanging in the closet.

He slowly turned his body so it was facing into his room, and his head turned toward Bonnie and Lauralei still standing near the front door. They both smiled and nodded.

Some of the tension left his body, and he stepped into the bedroom and went to the toy box on his left. He opened the top and began looking through the contents, making a mental inventory.

Bonnie and Lauralei had moved to the bedroom doorway and watched Curtis examining each toy in the box. After he had accounted for each one, he turned toward the two women. The corners of his mouth moved upward into a contented smile.

Bonnie's relief was such that she felt her knees go wobbly.

Chapter 10

Lauralei continued taking Curtis to ESD classes in Laramie when she went to work. In the meantime, Bonnie spent her days trying to find a job in Albany and Centennial; and she even made some trips to Laramie in search of work. But her recent past seemed to follow her.

Every place she put in an application knew she had been arrested, and even though all changes were dropped they all knew that she had, in fact, killed her husband. They weren't interested in the circumstances – the fact that she had been defending herself and her son. No business owner was willing to employ someone with that in their background.

During her time at home, she did all she could to keep her rising anxiety from showing, at least to Curtis. While he was not so with his mother or Lauralei, he continued to be withdrawn with others. Very little changed in his attitude with his teacher and the other students in the ESD classroom. Daniel had been able to give him some one-on-one attention for about an hour a day, but his behavior remained the same.

The bright spot was that his quizzes and tests remained higher than the other students.

"He is an exceptionally bright boy," Daniel told Bonnie during a visit she made to the ESD facility while in Laramie filling out job applications. "But he continues to isolate himself from the other students, and from me."

Bonnie had never shared with anyone Curtis' involvement in Delgado's death. While he had insisted in his interviews with the police at the time that he had killed the man, Bonnie denied it and her story that she had administered each wound to her husband never changed. But Daniel did know all the other details about the incident.

"What do you think it is that is making him this way?" Bonnie asked.

He thought for a moment or two before answering.

"I'm not a psychologist, but in my experience with young children who have been through traumatic events like Curtis has, they tend to avoid conversation that could lead them to relive the events," Daniel said. "But Curtis' case seems more intense than others I've seen."

She guessed the reason for that increased intensity was Curtis' involvement in the killing. But she kept the guess to herself.

"Is there anything that can be done to help him?" Bonnie asked.

"My best advice is to be his mother, be there for him," Daniel said. "It could take some time, but I think eventually he will come out of this."

Bonnie turned Delgado's two-year-old Ford F-250 onto the street on which her house was located. She had kept the truck because it was more reliable than her own car, which she had sold a few weeks before to get some cash. She got twenty-five hundred dollars for the car, and she felt lucky to have gotten that amount.

She was running through her mind all the places she had gone for job applications, and it was a few seconds before she realized there was an unfamiliar car in front of her home. She tapped on the brakes and pulled to the curb. The non-descript sedan was not running, but Bonnie noticed two men sitting in the front seats. She also noticed the U.S. government license plate on the rear of the vehicle.

Bonnie pulled the truck back onto the street and drove past the car to park in front of it. As she passed, she recognized Neil Cole, the DEA agent who had tried to interview her while she was in jail, sitting in the driver's seat. The height of her truck would not allow her to see who was in the passenger seat, but she guessed it was Cole's partner, Raymond Peck.

Bonnie climbed out of the truck and walked between it and the DEA car. She watched the two men inside the entire way, an angry scowl on her face. They, in turn, had the blank, unreadable look on their faces she remembered from the jail. When she reached the sidewalk, she turned her head toward the house as she headed for the front door. But she heard two car doors open. Bonnie's anger boiled over and she whirled around to face the agents advancing toward her.

"I told the police I don't know anything about what my husband was into," she hissed at them. "Now leave me the hell alone."

The agents stopped dead in their tracks at her first words. But their expressions did not change.

"Ms. Delga… " Cole began, but stopped himself. "Ms. Herden, we find it hard to believe you were married to the man and you had no clue about what he was doing. It's no different than when we interviewed you before."

Bonnie pulled her cell phone from her purse and scrolled through her recent calls, selecting a contact and pressing the call button.

"You know who my lawyer is; you need to talk to her," she said as she put the phone to her ear.

"We have already spoken to her," Peck said. "But we have an investigation to continue, and we know you can help us. She agreed with us."

Bonnie hesitated when Peck said they had talked to Holly. She did not hear her attorney say hello until the third utterance.

"Bonnie, is that you?" Holly asked.

"Yes, it's me," Bonnie said when she snapped out of her daze. "Those DEA agents are here accusing me of knowing what that man was into. They said they already talked to you about it and you agreed that I knew what they want."

"Bonnie, where are you?" Holly asked. Bonnie could hear anger in her voice.

"I'm standing in front of my house and those guys are right in front of me," she answered.

"Go into the house, don't let them in, lock the door and don't open it until I get there," Holly said.

Bonnie turned on her heel and jogged to the door. Once inside, she locked the knob and the dead bolt when she shut the door behind her. The two DEA agents were still standing on the sidewalk where she had left them.

Neither Lauralei nor Curtis were home.

Thirty minutes later, Holly's purple Dodge Challenger parked at the curb behind the DEA agents' car with an Albany County Sheriff's Office patrol car right behind her. Bonnie had stood at the picture window peeking through a small opening from the curtains she had pulled aside the entire thirty minutes since coming into the house. Cole and Peck also remained in front of the house during that time. They had been leaning against their car chatting until Holly's and the sheriff's car pulled up. Holly exited her car and Sheriff Moore got out of the patrol car. They approached the DEA agents, talking as they fast-walked toward them.

Bonnie could not make out all the words that were exchanged, but she could certainly see that both Holly and Sheriff Moore were angry. They alternated speaking and the agents tried to interject from time to time. But they didn't seem to be able to get a few words out before either Holly or the sheriff cut them off.

After a few moments, the sheriff pulled a document from the pocket inside his jacket and handed it to Cole. He glanced at the papers and seemed to argue with the sheriff. But Moore was having none of it. With his left hand he pointed at the agents' car and he rested his right hand on the 1911 Colt in its holster at his hip.

The agents stood there silently for a few seconds. Then Peck put his arm on Cole's shoulder and gently guided him toward the street. Cole crossed the front of the car and opened the driver's side door as Peck slid into the passenger seat. Cole hollered a few words over the top of the car before getting in and starting the engine. He then roared away, scattering dust and small pebbles in his wake, leaving Holly and Sheriff Moore fanning the air. Moore talked into the mic clipped to his shoulder as Holly headed for the front door. When the sheriff was finished on the radio, he followed the lawyer.

Bonnie had the door open before they reached it.

"Thank you for coming," she said, glancing at both Holly and the sheriff. She invited them in and they went inside.

"Are you okay?" Holly asked.

"Just a little rattled and pissed," Bonnie said. "I don't know anything about what my ex was involved in. I didn't even know what it was until I was arrested."

Bonnie sat on the ratty leather recliner, facing diagonally across the room toward the television on the wall opposite the chair. Holly and the sheriff seated themselves on the sofa with its back to the wall opposite the picture window.

"We've got them off your back for now, but it may not last long," the sheriff said.

Holly explained that before she left Laramie, she had filed a restraining order prohibiting the agents from having any contact with Bonnie in person, over the phone, through the mail or any other means. The order restricted them from being within five hundred feet of her.

But there was a catch.

"Since they are federal agents, if they challenge the order, it won't hold water in court," Holly said.

"And I suspect they will challenge it," the sheriff said. "The last thing Cole said was, 'This is not over.'"

"So, they'll keep harassing me?" Bonnie asked, her anger mixed with fear.

"That's very likely," Holly said. "But don't worry, I'll keep doing what I can to keep them from bothering you," she quickly added when she saw Bonnie go pale.

"Why did you tell them I knew what that man was involved in?" Bonnie asked, looking at Holly. Her trust in the attorney was suddenly in question.

"Bonnie, I didn't tell them any such thing," Holly said, trying to hide her disgust for the federal agents. "They were trying to trick you into talking."

The explanation seemed to restore trust in Holly, but Bonnie put her face in her hands and sobbed, as silently as she could. She was fighting hard not to show weakness, but she was losing the battle.

Holly and the sheriff were a little uncomfortable watching her struggle. Holly almost got up to go comfort her client, but held back. She knew Bonnie had been through a lot already. But she did not want her to lose that resolve she had seen her display in the jail interview after she had prodded her.

"I can't afford an attorney. I don't know how I'm going to pay you for what you've already done," she said after composing herself.

"Don't worry about any of that," Holly said. "We'll work that out."

But she had already decided she would handle any of Bonnie's legal needs pro bono. However, she did not want to say that in front of the sheriff. In addition to her public defender work with the county, she had begun taking some cases on her own time to lay the foundation for a private practice. She didn't want her willingness to do some work free of charge to get around the county rumor mill. She hadn't done any pro bono work so far in her young career. Not that she never would. But she wanted to pick her own cases, not have to fend off every hard luck case in the county.

Sheriff Moore scooted forward on the sofa, perching right on the edge, and leaned forward. He dropped his head to look at the floor for a few seconds. When his head came up to look straight at Bonnie, she felt her heart rate quicken. Moore had a look on his face that conveyed the deepest concern.

"The DEA agents continuing to harass you will be the least of your worries," he said in a tone that nearly made the blood freeze in Bonnie's veins. She glanced at Holly, whose own facial expression carried the same concern.

"Your former husband was in business with some very bad people," the sheriff continued. "They will no doubt have the same outlook the DEA has – that you knew what he was into."

Moore paused for a moment to let that sink in. In that moment, Bonnie became alarmed. But not about her own safety. She was more worried about Curtis. She knew nothing about Delgado's illegal activities, although she was not entirely surprised to have learned what they were. She had suspected for some time that he was capable of some shady dealings.

Bonnie was certain the sheriff's warning meant whoever Delgado had been working with would be concerned she would go to the authorities with what they thought she knew. They might even think she had already done so during her incarceration. She had watched enough true crime stories on television to know criminals would try to silence her.

But she was less worried about what they might do to her to get that done than what they might do to her son to coerce her silence.

"I don't know what they want," Bonnie said, shaking her head as she looked to the floor. "How can I make them understand that?"

"You can't," the sheriff said. "They want what they want and they'll do whatever it takes to get it."

Bonnie slowly lifted her head and looked straight into the sheriff's eyes.

"To me and anyone I care about." It was not a question. Moore slowly nodded his head.

An icy quiet enveloped the house. It hung in the air like a San Francisco Bay fog for a few uncomfortable moments. Bonnie finally broke the silence.

"What can I do to protect myself?" she asked.

Holly and the sheriff exchanged a glance.

"You should get yourself and your son out of Albany County," Moore said. "Maybe even out of Wyoming."

"I'll really miss you if you leave," Lauralei told Bonnie as they sat in their living room. "I'll miss Curtis, too."

Lauralei and Bonnie had been friends for years and there was a strong bond. While she had known Curtis since his birth, Lauralei had become quite attached to the boy in the time she had driven him to and from school while Bonnie was incarcerated and in the weeks she had been working in Laramie and Curtis was going to the ESD there.

She had no children of her own, and that was by her own choice. But spending time with Curtis stirred the motherly instincts in her. She enjoyed the time she spent with the boy, even as troubled as he was.

"We'll miss you, too," Bonnie replied. "But I haven't made any decision about leaving."

Lauralei reached across the couch and laid her hand on Bonnie's.

"But the sheriff said you could be in danger here," she said.

Bonnie slowly nodded.

"Yes, he did hint at that," she said. "But in all this time since…" Bonnie stopped in mid-sentence as the memories of that fateful night just down the hall flooded her mind. But it was more than that. She could not bring herself to speak the name of her second husband. Lauralei squeezed her friend's hand, hoping she got the message that her reluctance to say Delgado's name was understood.

"Nothing has happened; no one has done anything to me or even tried to talk to me," she said.

"But that's not to say something won't happen," Lauralei said.

Bonnie glanced down the hallway and stayed silent for a few seconds. Curtis was in their bedroom playing. His mother was curious to know whether he could hear the two women's conversation. She also wondered what Curtis' reaction would be to going away. She could hear muffled noises from the bedroom, the toy cars and trucks being pushed across the carpet and Curtis' imitation of the engine noises.

"That's true," Bonnie finally said. "But if we left, where would we go?"

Following Bonnie's graduation from high school, her parents departed Wyoming to take a trip to Europe they had saved money and planned for. It was to be the honeymoon they never had when they married because they were struggling college students at the time. But their jetliner from New York to London had exploded in mid-air over the North Atlantic Ocean, and there were no survivors.

They had no other children, so Bonnie had no siblings. All Bonnie's grandparents had died of natural causes at relatively young ages while she was in grade school. Her extended family – uncles, aunts, cousins – were far-flung across the country and Bonnie had not had contact with any of them since after her parents' deaths. Bonnie had rarely been out of Wyoming.

Aside from Lauralei and Curtis, Bonnie had no one in her life.

Her friend's voice snapped Bonnie out of her reflective thoughts.

"What about Nebraska?" she asked.

Bonnie was taken aback. Why on Earth would Lauralei suggest Nebraska? The look on Bonnie's face conveyed her confusion.

"You once told me that your parents had owned a house in some podunk town there and you ended up getting it when they died," Lauralei said.

That jogged Bonnie's memory. She hadn't thought of that property in some time, and with recent circumstances it was even further from her mind. It had been in her parents' will but it was only a couple of months after she lost her parents that the property deed was conveyed over to her in accordance with her parents' wills. She had it tucked away somewhere in her things.

Her parents had been renting out the house and the proceeds from that, less an amount for a caretaker to look after the property and manage the renters, were put into a trust fund for Bonnie when she had children. The fund was set up so the money was automatically deposited by the caretaker and the trust could not be accessed until Bonnie's first child was 18.

Bonnie and her parents were listed as the trustees. But after their deaths, Bonnie had not added anyone else as trustees, not even Vince – and certainly not Delgado, whom Bonnie had never told about the trust. In the last nine years, she had talked with the property's caretaker from time to time, but only when he called to get permission to make repairs on the house. She had not heard from him in more than a year.

"Why would I go there?" she asked. She couldn't remember the name of the town the property was in, nor where in the state it was located.

"It is away from here and those guys he was involved with," Lauralei said, avoiding saying Delgado's name out of respect for her friend.

"It's not that far away," Bonnie said. "And after all this time, what condition would the house be in? I've never even been there, as far as I remember."

"I think it would be worth at least looking into," Lauralei said.

"Like I said, I haven't even made a decision to go anywhere," Bonnie said. "What the sheriff thinks might happen may never happen."

However, despite what she told her friend, there was a part of Bonnie's mind that was tossing the idea around.

Chapter 11

Bonnie was loading some groceries into the back of the truck in the store parking lot. She felt guilty letting Lauralei pay all the household expenses. So she dipped into the money she had gotten from her car and bought a couple of months' worth of food and other items. School was out, and Curtis was sitting in the passenger seat of the truck playing a game on his mother's cell phone.

Done loading, she pushed the shopping cart to the nearest cart corral and walked toward the truck. As she reached the left side back panel, two men approached her from the cars parked beside her truck.

One man was about her height, but his torso was the shape of a wooden whiskey barrel. His skin was dark brown. If not for the facial features, which included a pencil-thin mustache, he could have been a black man. His companion, a white man, was taller, about six inches more than Bonnie, and thin. This guy was fidgety, whereas his partner was very self-assured.

"Hey, Chica, you've got something that belongs to us and we want it back," the shorter man said.

Their sudden appearance startled Bonnie. Without thinking, she glanced into the cab to ensure Curtis was safely inside. The tall man noticed and went to the driver's side door and tried to open it. But the door was locked. As was her practice when Curtis was with her, she left the key fob in the truck with him, instructing him to unlock it when she was ready to load then lock it again when she closed the bed cover and tailgate. He would then unlock the doors when she was ready to get in.

"I don't have anything that belongs to you," Bonnie said, and tried to walk away from the truck. She wanted to go into the store and use a phone there to call the police. But the two men stopped her, the short man grabbing her arm and pushing her against the side of the truck.

"Oh yes you do, Chica," The short man said. "Delgado was holding out on us. We want what he owes us."

Bonnie tried to pull away, but he squeezed her arm tighter. Despite trying to stay as calm as she could, he was hurting her and she yelped loudly.

In the truck, Curtis heard his mother and looked at the driver's side mirror. He saw the two men pressing in on her as she was pinned against the side of the truck. He quickly exited the game he was playing, pressed the call button and dialed 911.

"This is 911; what is your emergency?" a calm female voice asked.

"My mother is being attacked by two men; she needs help," Curtis said.

The operator could tell she was talking to a young boy. She knew it was doubly important to keep him calm so she could gather all the information she could.

"What is your name?" she asked.

"Curtis," he said. "Please help us."

"My name is Melanie. How old are you, Curtis?" she asked.

"I'm seven," he said.

"Where are you located?" the woman asked.

"We're at the store," Curtis said.

"What store? In what town?" the operator asked, still calm.

"The grocery store in Albany," he answered.

Curtis could hear the short man's voice getting louder and more insistent. He had the presence of mind not to turn his head to look in their direction. Instead, he watched the side mirror, with an occasional glance at the rearview mirror.

"Is your mother in the store?" the operator asked.

"No, we're outside," Curtis informed her.

"Curtis, are you next to your mother?" the operator asked.

"No, I'm in the truck and she's outside," Curtis said.

"Okay, since you're in the truck, I want you to put the phone on speaker. Do you know how to do that?" The dispatcher asked.

"Yes," Curtis said, then hit the button for the speaker and took the phone from his ear and held it in his lap.

"I'm going to speak in a low voice but you should still be able to hear me. When you answer, speak softly so the men don't hear you, and hold the phone like you are playing games on it, okay," she instructed. He acknowledged her.

"What kind of truck are you in?" Melanie asked.

"It's blue," he said.

"Curtis, do you know what make or model the truck is?" Melanie asked, believing most boys in Wyoming knew their trucks.

"I don't know," he said.

"Is your mother and the men near the truck?" she asked.

"They are at the back," Curtis said. "The short man is holding her arm. I think he's hurting her. I heard her yell."

Outside the truck, the tall man looked into the truck cab.

"The kid is on the phone," he said to the short man.

"What is he doing?" the short man asked, getting close to Bonnie's face, so close she could smell the guacamole on his breath.

"He's playing games on my phone," Bonnie answered. The short man stared at her for a few seconds, but found no trace of deceit.

"That better be all he is doing, Chica," he said, giving her arm one last squeeze then letting it go. "We want what your husband kept from us. So, you better tell us where we can find it."

Suddenly, they all heard the roar of a high-powered engine then the squeal of tires as brakes were applied. A sheriff's patrol car was stopped in back of the truck and two deputies jumped out, the one from the passenger side with his hand on his holstered revolver.

"What's the problem here?" the deputy from the driver's side asked.

"No problem, officer," the short man said.

"Yes, there is," Bonnie said, shuffling away from the back of the truck to the driver's side door. "These guys were harassing me."

The tall man stiffened and reached behind him. Bonnie looked and saw a pistol tucked into the back of his jeans. Just as his hand closed on the grip, both deputies pulled their Glocks from the holsters and pointed them at the tall man.

"Don't even think about it, buster," the lead deputy said.

Bonnie dived to the ground and rolled under the truck. Unfazed by the firearms being raised in his direction, the tall man completed pulling the pistol from his pants and started to swing his arm up. He got it about halfway to firing position when two sheriff's deputies' pistols barked twice each.

Almost simultaneously, four slugs impacted the tall man's chest center mass. One ricocheted off his breastplate and went directly through his heart. A second passed through two ribs and hit his spine, shattering two vertebrae. A third ripped through the right lung, exiting through the back rib cage at a low enough velocity to drop harmlessly on the pavement. The fourth bullet was a through-and-through that bounced off the hood of the car parked right behind him and striking the right windshield post.

The 911 operator had just told Curtis that sheriff's deputies just pulled up when she heard the gunshots.

"What was that, Curtis?" she asked with a little bit of alarm in her voice.

"One of the guys got shot," he answered in a tone so calm it shocked the dispatcher.

The bullet impacts had thrown the tall man half onto the hood of the car behind him, but he slowly slid off to a sitting position in front of the grill. His sliding body left a trail of blood. His head had flopped to the left, and his lifeless eyes stared at Bonnie. His gun had dropped from his right hand and was on the pavement near his foot.

The lead deputy quickly holstered his weapon while the other kept the short man covered. The handcuffs were securely fastened and he was led back to the patrol car. As Bonnie rolled out from under the truck, the short man looked over his shoulder and glared at her. The lead deputy roughly tossed him in the back seat of the car, not bothering to cover the man's head to keep him from bumping it on the doorframe.

Bonnie and Curtis sat silently in Albany County Sheriff Jesse Moore's office. They had just completed giving their statements about what happened in the grocery store parking lot. Bonnie was exhausted, both from giving her statement and the events themselves. Curtis, however, seemed none the worse for the experience. He sat at his mother's side, calmly reading a book about a fictional Wyoming county sheriff Moore had handed him when they came into the sheriff's office substation.

But Bonnie was not just exhausted. She was very frightened.

The encounter with the two men and the violent way it ended pounded home just how much danger she and her son were in. Even though one of the men was dead and the other cooling his heels in the county jail, Bonnie was certain they would not be the only ones to come after her.

In addition to the fear, she was also frustrated. She knew nothing about what her second husband was involved in. She only heard about it when she went to jail for killing him.

How could she make the rest of the thugs that would be after her understand that? And the events in the parking lot brought up another scary question. The Mexican man with the thin mustache had said something about her having something that belonged to them and they wanted it back. That could only mean that her second husband either stole something from those who sent the pair to threaten her and Curtis or he was holding out on them.

What could it have been? She was savvy enough to know that since he was smuggling drugs, it was either that or money that someone wanted returned. He had also been involved in human trafficking, but there was no way he could have hidden people. Or could he?

Knowing now what she knew about her second husband, Bonnie decided that anything was possible. But knowing that did not get her off the hook with whoever was after whatever it was they were after.

Her thoughts were interrupted when the sheriff walked into his office.

"Well, we've gotten your statements recorded," Moore said as he sat in his basic chair behind his desk. "All the other witnesses, including the deputies, tell the same version, with a few insignificant variations."

He paused for a moment, looking from Bonnie to Curtis. The boy's attention was riveted on the book while his mother looked straight ahead. Moore could see the fear in her eyes.

"Is there anything else you want to add to any of this?" the sheriff asked.

A bit of anger creeped into Bonnie's expression.

"You mean, what am I hiding?" she spat.

The sheriff put his elbows on the desk, cupped his hands together, steepled his index fingers and rested them against his chin. He studied Bonnie for a few seconds, looking for any signs of deception. There were none.

"It would be nice if you were hiding something and told me about it," he said with his fingers still on his chin, then he dropped his hands to the top of his desk and sighed. "But I don't think you're holding anything back."

Bonnie's expression relaxed, but only slightly. The fear was still strong in her.

"But while that means I won't be pressing you for anything doesn't mean the pressure's off for you," the sheriff said.

Bonnie silently agreed.

"What should I do?" Bonnie asked, but she knew what the answer would be.

"My advice remains the same," the sheriff said. "I think you need to get out of Wyoming."

"Won't they just follow me?" Bonnie asked.

"It depends on where you go and what you do when you get there," the sheriff said.

"What do you mean?" she asked.

"You've got to put some distance between yourself and here," the sheriff said. "Find a small out-of-the-way place in another state. And don't make waves, don't put your name out there, stay under the radar, as they say."

Bonnie sat silently for a moment, thinking about what she and Lauralei had talked about before the incident at the store.

It was at that point that Holly tapped on the sheriff's office door and he motioned for her to enter.

"I came as soon as you called," she told the sheriff, then went to Bonnie's side. "How are you doing?"

"I'm okay, a little scared," she answered.

"I'm advising Bonnie to leave Wyoming," the sheriff said. "I'm doing that for her protection," he added when Holly started to protest. She had neither agreed nor disagreed when Moore suggested that at Bonnie's house. On one hand she saw the logic in the advice, but on the other, she knew it would be a difficult endeavor for Bonnie to make such a move.

"She should put some distance between her and this situation and the people her former husband was involved with," Moore said.

Holly looked at Bonnie.

"I think it might be a good idea," Bonnie said, answering her attorney's unspoken question.

"The trouble is, Bonnie's not in a financial position to make such a major move," Holly said.

"I believe the county could help with that," the sheriff said.

When Holly told the sheriff Bonnie was not in a financial position to make a major move, that did not mean she was destitute. When her parents died, there was a small nest egg available for Bonnie after all their debts were paid off. Since their bodies were never found after the airliner explosion, there were no funeral or burial expenses. But they had some credit card debts related to their unrealized vacation plans. They had also put a down payment on a house, none of which was returned to the estate when the sale was not consummated.

Bonnie had put the money she got from her parents' estate into a saving account, which she had intended to use for her college education. While some of it was consumed paying expenses related to Vince's death, some still remained. She continued to keep those funds there, only dipping into them in the most dire emergencies. She had kept the account's existence a secret from her second husband.

After being released from jail, she had used some of the money to live on until Lauralei moved into her rented home and took over the household expenses. With no means of steady income, Holly advised her to keep the money in the savings account until she made the move, then it could be used to live on until she got a job in the new location.

Now it was time to make a decision about where it was she wanted to relocate. It was not a hard decision to make.

Bonnie dug through her belongings in the master bedroom closet at the Albany rental house. The deed to the Nebraska house had been another secret she kept from Delgado. Like her savings account, she feared he would find a way to get his hands on it and waste it away, leaving her with nothing.

It had been so long since she had hidden the deed, and she had hidden it so well, that it took her a while to find it. But after pulling everything out of the closet in preparation for packing it up, she saw the metal ring on the carpet in the corner of the closet. Around it was a very faint outline in the carpet, two feet on each side. It was the access to the crawl space under the house.

Bonnie put her finger in the ring and gently pulled upward. It didn't budge, so she pulled harder and it grudgingly gave way. She pulled it completely up and leaned it against the wall. She peered down into the hole and saw nothing but black.

Suddenly, two points of yellowish-white light appeared in the darkness a little farther back from the hole.

"Curtis, bring me a flashlight," she yelled. The tiny lights moved a little backward.

After a moment, Curtis was at her side with a small tubular flashlight. She switched it on and shined it toward the lights. Staring back at her was a small furry animal. The black outlines around its eyes made it look like Robin from the old Batman TV series.

"Shoo," Bonnie said, waving the flashlight inside the hole. The raccoon backed up several more steps and continued staring up into the open hole and the bright light.

Bonnie pointed the flashlight to the left and saw the small shelf she had nailed to the floor of the house those years ago. On the shelf was the small metal box she had placed there. She reached in and took it from the shelf, the raccoon watching her every move. When she had the box on the closet floor, she put the cover back over the hole.

Taking the box to the kitchen, with Curtis following closely behind, Bonnie dusted it off over the kitchen sink. Setting it on the counter, she went to her purse and retrieved her keys. Selecting a small, thin one, she inserted it into the lock on the box and turned it until she felt the tab slip off the locking plate.

Lifting the box lid, Bonnie saw the regular business-size envelope inside. With it were two identical keys on a small wire ring. She took out the envelope and opened the unsealed flap. She removed the single quad-folded paper inside and opened it to its full size. The gold design around the edges framed a barely distinguishable blue background with typewritten descriptions in the middle. She glanced to the bottom and saw the words converting the deed from her parents to her. She ran her fingers across their signatures. The date was a week before they departed on their trans-ocean vacation.

Bonnie then looked up at the property description. It was a one-acre property with one dwelling unit located in the southeastern corner within the boundaries of a Nebraska town.

Hazard.

"What's that, Mom," she heard Curtis ask from her side.

After a short pause, she said, "That's our new home."

Chapter 12

Bonnie and Lauralei sat in two chairs in front of Sheriff Jesse Moore's desk. Curtis was next to his mother on a small stool the sheriff had brought in from the bullpen, where several desks stood ready for deputies when they came in to write reports and perform other duties when they were not on patrol. He was reading a different book he had found on a shelf in the sheriff's office.

Moore had asked the two women to come in to discuss Bonnie's and Curtis' imminent departure for Nebraska. As it turned out, the house Bonnie now owned in Hazard, Nebraska, had been empty for almost two months. The people who were renting the home had been arrested on drug charges. Once they got out of jail, they quickly packed up their belongings and disappeared.

Bonnie's talk with the caretaker revealed that when those renters made their getaway, they left some damage in the house, and the repairs were nearly complete. She was told he was ready to place an ad in local newspapers and on social media that the house was now available for rent.

"Don't put it up for rent," Bonnie told him. "My son and I are going over there to live. We'll be living in the house."

She made arrangements with the caretaker to continue maintaining the property and she would keep paying him for the service, at a bit of a lower rate since he would no longer be responsible for making sure there were renters in the home.

Bonnie and Curtis planned to leave within the week. But Sheriff Moore was convinced that since the two who had approached Bonnie in the store parking lot mentioned they believed Bonnie's former husband had something that belonged to them, whoever they were, that those people would continue to come after her.

"So, what we want to do is search your truck and house to see if we can find what it is they are after," Moore said.

"And what happens if you do find something?" Bonnie asked.

"We'll confiscate it, of course, and make sure the word gets around that we have it," Moore explained. "If they know we have it, we're sure they will leave you alone."

"What do you think you might find?" Lauralei asked.

"Well, it will most likely be drugs or money – or both," the sheriff said.

That made sense to both women. But Bonnie knew her second dead husband was involved in more than the drug trade.

"But what about the human smuggling I was told he was into?" Bonnie asked.

The sheriff's puzzled look almost made Lauralei burst out laughing, but she controlled herself.

"No, sheriff, I'm sure Bonnie doesn't think there are people stashed in the house or her truck," she said. "But they may think she knows something about that activity that could be bad for them."

Moore chuckled a little.

"Okay, I understand," he said. "And I suppose that is a possibility."

He raised his hand when he saw the alarmed look on Bonnie's face.

"I said it's a possibility," he said. "But I think it's a slim possibility. If you are not here any longer, you'd really not be much of a danger to them."

"Maybe," Lauralei said. "But what if they come looking for her at the house here? That's where I'll be."

"We'll be watching your house closely," the sheriff said.

"Maybe for a while. But sooner or later, you'll lose interest," Lauralei said a little testily.

Moore was a little stung by the jab, but he did not show it outwardly, mostly because she was right.

"Eventually, when we believe enough time has passed that they have lost interest, we will scale back extra patrols past your house," he said calmly. "But until that time comes, we will watch out for you." Lauralei's angry demeaner seemed to dissipate a little. "And after that, we are only a phone call away," he added, pointing to his cell phone on the desk in front of him.

"She didn't mean any disrespect," Bonnie said. Lauralei shot her friend a thankful glance. "She's just worried, and so am I."

"I understand, and we'll do everything we can to ensure your safety," Moore said. "That includes alerting law enforcement in Sherman County over in Nebraska."

Bonnie felt relieved. She glanced at her son for the first time since their conversation with the sheriff had begun. Curtis was still reading, seemingly totally engrossed in the book. But in addition to reading, the boy had been listening intently to the two women and the sheriff.

"Now, if you agree, we'll begin the search of your truck and the house," the sheriff said. "We'll do a careful search of both, but we won't damage anything."

Bonnie and Lauralei gave their consent.

Moore instructed Bonnie to take her Ford F-250 pickup to a dealership in Laramie. He had two deputies dressed as technicians standing by. Under the guise of having the vehicle serviced for the road trip to Nebraska, the deputies searched the vehicle within the secured confines of the dealership's service department.

The sheriff was aware that Bonnie could be under watch by those whom Delgado had been working for. He did not want to let them know her truck and house were being searched.

For the house, two more deputies in casual plain clothes went to the house in Albany. They greeted Lauralei at the door as if they were old friends coming for a visit. She invited them inside and they went to work.

With both the house and truck, deputies were ordered to do a very thorough search, but not to the extent of tearing either apart. Moore was conscious that Bonnie needed the truck for her personal transportation and Lauralei was going to continue living in the house. He suspected neither woman of any wrongdoing, so he did not want to disrupt their lives any more than he had to.

During both searches, special equipment was used to X-ray through walls and floors. Getting the equipment undetected into the dealership was easier than at the house. But for the latter, Moore had it packaged and delivered through a major carrier as if Lauralei were receiving a package.

The three-hour manual search and X-ray equipment yielded no results for the truck. But things were different at the house.

After the initial manual search of the interior, they used the X-ray and discovered what appeared to be something stored in the crawl space under the house. The deputies relayed that information to the sheriff, who called Bonnie waiting at the Laramie dealership.

"Is there anything stored in the crawl space under the house?" he asked.

"No," she said after a few seconds' thought. "The only thing I know of was a metal box that had the deed to the Nebraska house. But I took that out."

"Can we access the crawl space from inside the house?" Moore asked. He did not want the deputies going under the house from the outside in view of any potential watchers.

"In the left corner of the closet in my bedroom, there is a kind of lid over an opening," she said. "There is a ring that you use to lift it."

One of the deputies went into the crawl space and found three large garbage bags tucked into a corner of the crawl space. They had been hidden behind sheets of plywood wedged between the floor and ground, no doubt to keep rodents and small animals away from them. Two of them were stuffed full and closed with twist ties. The third bag was about one-third full and also closed with a twist tie. He opened each bag. Inside were tightly wrapped, brick-shaped bundles rounded at the edges. He pulled one out, used his utility knife to cut it open and, using his flashlight, looked inside.

"We've got a mix of cocaine and heroin in two full large landscape garbage bags and another one that is about one-third full," Deputy Sam Bullock, after inspection of other bricks, told the sheriff when he had come up from the crawl space. "We counted 215 bricks."

"Holy shit," the sheriff said. "That's a lot of drugs. Do you think he was distributing it from the house?"

"I don't think so," Bullock said. "I didn't see anything down there that indicated any of it was going out, just that he was adding to a stash."

"So, it's likely he was skimming from his bosses," Moore said. "He may have been getting ready to sell it during one of his long hauls."

Getting the X-ray equipment out of the house without suspicion was easy enough. It was repacked in the same box it was delivered in and the same carrier came to pick it up, as if Lauralei was dissatisfied with her order and was returning it.

Removing the drugs was a little tougher. But Sheriff Moore decided not to put together a complicated plan. The simplest and most normal was the best shot.

A few days later, a different deputy, dressed for the part, accompanied a solid waste truck driver as he drove up in a solid waste truck during the normal pickup day for that area of town. Lauralei had her trash can at the curb and when she saw the truck coming toward the house, she carried the garbage bags of drugs, one at a time, out and set them next to the trash container.

The truck driver operated the pickup arm for the container while the disguised deputy grabbed the bags and put them in the back of the truck. Lauralei made sure not to wave at the vehicle as it headed down the street to finish the route. The driver was told not to compact his load this time. When the truck returned to the company's headquarters, the deputy transferred the bags into an unmarked pickup, and they were taken to the county sheriff's evidence locker.

Moore was satisfied the operation was completed without giving anything away to anyone who might have been watching.

He planned to loop the DEA into what they had found once Bonnie was well on her way to Nebraska.

"There is a little over sixty thousand dollars in the trust your parents set up for Curtis," Holly told Bonnie. "It still lists you and your parents as the trustees. That should be updated."

Bonnie had gone to see Holly to wrap up a few things before she made the move to Nebraska. She had not intended to do anything about the trust. After all, she hadn't done anything about it since she found out it existed, so she believed nothing needed to be done until it was time to close it.

What she had wanted to clear up with Holly's help was to make sure there were no more reasons for her to be staying in Albany. Considering her earlier arrest and time in jail, she believed there might be some lingering reason for law enforcement or the court to keep her in Wyoming.

Holly assured her all the legal issues had been resolved. Except, of course, for the trust.

"Nothing was done before; why do I need to do something now?" Bonnie asked.

"The reason for having multiple people listed on a trust is to make sure that no one person can take the assets," Holly said. "Since the house in Nebraska was specifically identified as the revenue source for the trust, that is an asset and is also part of it."

"But the deed to the property was signed over to me," Bonnie said.

"And you are the owner of the property. But since it was listed as an asset in the trust, that just means you can't sell the property," Holly explained.

"I don't want to sell it," Bonnie said. "That's where I'm going to live."

"That is your intention now," Holly said. "But if sometime in the future you decide to live somewhere else, the house remains in the trust and reverts to a rental to provide revenue for the trust."

"So, since it feeds money into the trust, I'll have to pay rent on a house I own," Bonnie said, disappointment and frustration peppering her tone.

"No, that's not the case," Holly said. "There is a clause in the trust that says any time you or Curtis or both are residents of the home, no rent is to be charged."

Bonnie did not quite understand the legal complexities of the trust, but she realized that her parents were trying to cover any and all contingencies to make sure that any children Bonnie had in the future not only had a nest egg but a home as well.

"You need to take your parents off the trust since they are deceased," Holly said. "If not, you will be the only trustee alive and would not be able to administer it."

"So, what do I need to do?" Bonnie asked, although she had a pretty good idea what was needed.

"We need to add two people as trustees," Holly said. "Pick people you know you can trust, people who won't throw you under the bus."

"Can Curtis be one of them?" Bonnie asked.

"No, not until he is eighteen," Holly said.

Bonnie thought it over for a few minutes. There were only two logical choices.

"You and Lauralei," she said.

"Bonnie, you don't know me. I may not be the best choice," Holly said modestly.

"No, you are the best choice," Bonnie countered. "What if something comes up that is legal-related? I don't know anyone else to turn to on that."

Holly argued against it and offered to refer some attorneys in Nebraska who could advise her. But Bonnie insisted. When it came right down to it, Lauralei and Holly were the only two people she knew that she could trust without question. And wasn't that what Holly had told her to consider when picking trustees?

Chapter 13

Bonnie's and Curtis' new life began at six o'clock on a Wednesday morning as they bid a tearful goodbye – at least for Bonnie and Lauralei. Curtis shed no tears. Not that he wasn't going to miss his mother's friend, because he would. But Curtis believed that men didn't cry. And now, in his young mind, he was the man of the household.

The day before, Moore and Holly had said their goodbyes at the sheriff's office. Moore handed Bonnie a debit card.

"This is loaded with ten thousand dollars," he said. Bonnie gasped, shooting her hand to her mouth. After a moment's hesitation, she gingerly took the card with her other hand.

"This is to cover your expenses for a while, until you can get a job in Hazard or somewhere near there," the sheriff said. He looked to Holly when Bonnie's astonishment cleared, and a puzzled look took its place.

"This is money the county sets aside to help people in your circumstances," the lawyer fibbed, making an effort not to look at the sheriff. "It's like the witness protection program without actually being in the program."

In actuality, the county had contributed only twenty-five hundred dollars, mostly because Holly guilted the prosecutor's office into it for putting Bonnie through what they had. Holly, through her connections, found out about the conversation between the prosecutor and the governor. She suspected those two had put up the money themselves from their campaign funds, but she couldn't prove it, nor did she want to.

Sheriff Moore had found a similar amount in discretionary funds from his office and Holly had contributed the rest from her own pocket.

Holly had also made all the changes they discussed in the trust fund.

The thirty-five miles between Albany and Laramie were covered in silence. Bonnie's and Curtis' belongings, clothing and personal mementoes, were packed in the back of the truck. Bonnie had left the furnishings in the Albany home as the house in Hazard was already furnished. Hopefully, those were not damaged by the past renters. If so, she would use some of the money from the county to replace them. Eventually, when she was securely employed, she would add to what was there to make it more to her liking.

They stopped at a McDonald's near the on-ramp to Interstate 80 on the east side of Laramie to get breakfast. After topping off the truck's tank with gas at a nearby station, Bonnie guided the truck onto the southbound lane of I-80. In less than a mile, the freeway, also called the Dwight D. Eisenhower Highway, went through a series of changes of direction –

mostly southeast and due south – skirting the Laramie Mountains. By the time they passed the Martin Marietta Granite Canyon Quarry just north of the freeway, the roadway followed a nearly due easterly course.

Curtis had never been anywhere other than southeastern Wyoming his entire life, so the drive was an adventure of discovery for him. His head was on a swivel as the truck made the trek east. He could see the activity at the quarry and was fascinated. It was the same reaction when they passed a large Walmart distribution center on the western outskirts of Cheyenne. He saw a Lowe's distribution center on the other side of the Wyoming capitol city when they stopped at a Pilot Travel Center to again top off the truck's gas tank.

Bonnie vaguely remembered being in Nebraska when she was very young – younger than her son was now – but had never been back. Having never driven through the state, she was uncertain how often they would see gas stations, so filled up at each large city they went through. She made another gas stop in Pine Bluffs while still in Wyoming. Back on the freeway, when she passed the city's eastern edge, they passed from Wyoming into the state of Nebraska.

It was clear from the terrain ahead of them they had gone from the Rocky Mountains to the Great Plains. Nebraska was as flat as an ironing board to the left, right, and straight ahead.

Bonnie was a bit disappointed as she loved being near mountains. She had heard, of course, about the flat terrain in Nebraska, but she could not picture an area with no mountains – let alone small hills.

"Where did the mountains go, Mom," Curtis asked.

At first, Bonnie was a little startled. Those were the first words Curtis had uttered since the day before. Not that he was a chatterbug normally. Ever since the killing of Delgado, the words he spoke during a day could be counted without using all of one's fingers.

"They are behind us, Baby," she finally answered. "Nebraska is one of the states that are part of what is called the Great Plains."

"I remember that from school," he said, then returned to silently observing the scenery.

As they neared Kimball, Bonnie did not think they had gone far enough to really need gas, and she was sure they would come across a town large enough with a gas station. She passed up Dix and Potter for the same reason. But after going past the latter, she began to believe she made a mistake.

Just as she was trying to look for a place to cross the freeway median to go back and go north to Potter, she saw a mileage sign stating Sidney was not far ahead. She continued on.

"Are you getting hungry, Curtis?" she asked.

"Yeah," was all he said.

"We'll get gas in Sidney and get some lunch there, too," Bonnie said.

They had been on the road just over three hours and covered one hundred eighty-two miles to their new home and new life.

Bonnie sat across from Curtis at the small table at the Taco John's in Sidney. She had gotten directions when she filled the truck's gas tank at the Love's Travel Stop next to the freeway before making the short drive north to Sidney itself. It was Curtis' favorite fast food restaurant, but he didn't get to enjoy it as much as he would have liked because the closest one to his Albany home was in Laramie, thirty-five miles away. He had not been there since before Delgado was killed.

They ordered and began their meal in silence. But Curtis suddenly caught his mother's attention.

"Why are we moving?" Curtis asked. "Is it because of what I did?"

The questions caught Bonnie a little off guard and she misunderstood.

"It wasn't your fault you had to go to Laramie for school," Bonnie said.

The boy took a bite of his stuffed grilled taco and slowly and carefully chewed then swallowed. He then took a sip of his soft drink.

"No, I mean me stabbing that man," he said calmly, as if he were talking about a school field trip. The restaurant was not full, but there were some people sitting nearby and their attention perked up when Curtis spoke that sentence.

Bonnie froze in mid-bite of her taco salad. She could feel the blood drain from her face and imagined she looked as white as a kabuki dancer. She took her time chewing her bite of lettuce, meat, tomato and cheese. She was running possible answers through her head, trying to find the best one to put her son at ease. At the same time, it was not lost on her that he did not seem ill at ease.

"You didn't do that," Bonnie whispered, noticing the nearby diners giving them a side glance.

"Yes I did, right here," Curtis said, indicating his throat.

Bonnie put her index finger to her lips.

"Please lower your voice," she said.

He popped a potato ole into his mouth and followed it with another.

"But is that why we're moving?" he whispered.

Curtis had been present during all his mother's discussions with Sheriff Moore about leaving Albany County. While each time he had his face in a book, he was taking in every word.

Daniel, Curtis' ESD teacher in Laramie, was right, he was an exceptionally bright boy. He understood adult conversations and concepts much more than other children his age. He had shown that with his quizzes and exams both in school and at the ESD. He also displayed more attention to detail, which is why he knew what he could and should do during the altercation in the Albany store parking lot.

But to this point, no one had explained in detail to him what was happening and why. The drug and human smuggling was somewhat of a mystery to him. He desperately wanted that information to come from his mother.

"We are moving for a lot of reasons, but I would rather not talk about them here," she told him. "We'll talk in the truck when we get back on the road and I'll answer all the questions you have."

"Okay," Curtis said, visibly quite satisfied, as he attacked the rest of his meal.

For the next one hundred twenty miles, Bonnie explained the entire situation to her son, leaving nothing out. He paid rapt attention and asked a few questions from time to time.

Bonnie wasn't sure just how much of it he truly understood. She spoke to him like an adult and did not talk down to him.

Curtis took it all in calmly, soaking up his mother's words like a sponge. He did not really understand how drug and human trafficking worked and asked for an explanation.

"I only know what I've seen on television and read about," Bonnie answered. "But it is against the law."

"If you don't know about it, why do the bad guys want you?" he asked.

"He had things they wanted, and they thought I knew where they were," she replied, still unwilling to say Delgado's name aloud.

"Did you?" Curtis asked.

At first, Bonnie was hurt that he would ask such a thing. But then she remembered that she was talking to a seven-year-old. It wasn't really a matter that he suspected she was involved in the illegal activities that his stepfather was into. He was just a little boy trying to understand such a complicated turn of events in his life.

"No, I didn't know anything about what he was involved in," she said as neutrally as she could manage, hoping her initial hurt feelings would not show.

She then explained that the police had searched the truck and the house in Albany and what they had found.

"They think there is also some money he hid somewhere, but they didn't find any," she said.

With the past history covered, Curtis then wanted to know where they were going and what it would be like there. Bonnie explained about the house in Hazard and how she had come to be its owner.

"But I have never been there, or I might have been when I was younger than you and don't remember," she said. "But I do know it is a very small town, a lot like Albany."

However, Bonnie had done some Internet research on Hazard and the surrounding area and shared that with her son.

Hazard was established in 1886 when the Grand Island and Wyoming Central Railroad extended to that point. Now the town, which covered about one-quarter of a square mile, had a population that varied but was now listed as having seventy residents, according to the most recent census.

The town was located within Sherman County, which was almost dead center in the state at two thousand one hundred and six feet above sea level. The nearest large cities were Kearney, twenty-eight miles away, and Grand Island, forty-three miles away.

"Is there a school there?" Curtis asked.

"Not in Hazard," Bonnie answered. "It looks like you will go to a school in Loup City, about twenty miles from Hazard, or Litchfield, about eight miles away."

She could see the disappointment on his face. He was not fond of the bus rides to Centennial when he was in school there, Bonnie knew, and while it was a little different when he went to the ESD in Laramie, because Lauralei drove him there, he still did not like the travel.

But the disappointment faded from his look as he moved on to his next inquiry.

"Why do they call it Hazard?" he asked.

"I really don't know, Baby," Bonnie said as she saw the mileage sign stating the freeway exit to Ogallala was less than a mile away.

This was the longest stretch she had driven so far without getting gasoline. Although the truck's gas gauge showed that not even a quarter of the full tank from Sidney had been burned, she had no idea where the next gas would be available. It was time to top off the tank again.

As it turned out, she passed up Ogallala and the next three towns – Paxton, twenty-one miles away; Sutherland, another twelve miles; and Hershey, nine miles more. But by the time she had gone fourteen more miles, she decided that was pushing it, so she pulled into North Platte. They were just a few more hours away from their destination.

They pulled into North Platte and stopped at a travel center near the freeway. In addition to filling the gas tank, they each used the restroom, and Bonnie bought them both something to drink and some snacks. They were back on the road within thirty minutes.

Once she settled into the moderate traffic on the roadway, Bonnie noticed in the rearview mirror a dirty brown sedan come down the exit ramp. It was a familiar vehicle. She had seen it off and on ever since they left Laramie.

A car traveling in the same direction on one of the busiest interstate freeways in the country was not unusual. She had seen other cars behind them for long stretches. But none of them had stayed behind them this long. Some took exits and others slowly overtook them and just as slowly put distance between them.

There was also something else familiar about this vehicle, beyond that it had been behind them since Laramie. It was a car she had seen driving slowly past her house in Albany a couple of times per week since she had gotten out of jail.

Bonnie did the best she could to keep the anxiety building within her from showing. She did not want Curtis to become curious and start asking questions.

"Let's play a game," she said. "Let's see if we can identify what state cars are from by their license plates and see if we can see what the numbers are."

"Okay," Curtis said enthusiastically.

As cars went by them, they identified each plate's state of origin. Curtis got most of them before his mother. She had intended to let that happen, but quickly learned Curtis was quicker at the game than she had anticipated. That was good, as it allowed her to concentrate on the car behind them.

Twice, she slowed her speed, hoping the car would pass them so they could identify the plate. But each time, the vehicle slowed its pace as well. If there were any doubts in Bonnie's mind about whether the car was following them, that erased them. She decided to try another tactic.

"You are just too good at this, you're beating me," Bonnie said to her son. "I'm going to make this a little harder."

He looked at her with an expression of satisfaction.

"Look in the rearview mirror and tell me where that brown car is from and what the plate number is," she instructed. At the same time she slowed the truck drastically so the car gained on them. It came within about fifty feet of the truck's tailgate before the driver reacted and slowed his vehicle. That was enough for Curtis.

"It's Wyoming," he said. "There is a five, then the bucking horse, then two fives, a zero and a seven."

Bonnie committed the numbers to memory, smiling at her son's intelligence.

"You're just too good for me at this," she said. "We'll have to think of another game."

Bonnie didn't want to wait too long to make the call she had planned. While she and Curtis played twenty questions, she looked for an opportunity to get off the freeway. She did not want to make her call in the truck where Curtis could hear. But the only thing she came across was an exit to a rural road with no buildings near it. She was afraid of the following car pulling off the roadway with her and what could happen with no one around to see the result.

As she passed that exit, she saw a mileage sign that said Gothenburg was not far ahead. She continued on to the town's exit and pulled into a gas station. She saw the brown car take the exit as well and park about fifty feet away. Neither of the two men inside got out of the car.

"I need to go to the bathroom, do you?" Bonnie asked. Curtis shook his head. "Well, stay in the truck and do not unlock the doors. I have the key."

Bonnie went into the station and found a quiet corner and dialed Sheriff Jesse Moore's cell phone number. She explained what had been happening.

"Okay, get back on the freeway and keep going toward Hazard. I'll take care of it," he said.

By the time Bonnie rolled the truck into Hazard, it was nearly five o'clock in the evening. It was much later than she had expected, and later than it should have taken. But she had taken a different route than she had planned.

As she was approaching the exit from Interstate 80 to Lexington just north of the freeway, she received a call from Sheriff Moore instructing her to go into the city and call him back. When she did, he explained he had called the Nebraska State Patrol and told them to pull the brown sedan over on suspicion of drug trafficking.

"There happened to be a patrol car not far away and they got them," the sheriff said. "As luck would have it, when the staters searched the car, they found a duffel bag full of weed packed in little baggies."

Bonnie, who again had gone into a gas station to make the call, leaving Curtis in the locked truck, was relieved, not just because whoever was following her was found out but also that her suspicion that they were, in fact, following her was correct.

"They're not going to be following you anymore, they were arrested and the car impounded," Moore said.

"Does that mean we are safe?" she asked.

There was a short pause, which made Bonnie a little uneasy.

"I would say yes," the sheriff said with a note of caution in his voice. "But that is not to say someone else might eventually start looking for you again."

Bonnie started to say something, but the words caught in her throat.

"We got their drugs, but there may have been money your former husband was holding onto," Moore explained. "Whoever is behind this drug and human smuggling ring may also still think you know something about the operation."

"But I don't know anything," Bonnie said, holding back tears. "And if he was hiding money, he hid it so well even your people couldn't find it."

Bonnie, standing out of sight of her truck, peeked around a state lottery ticket dispensing machine and saw the truck out the window. Curtis was sitting patiently in the passenger seat. He was looking straight ahead through the windshield. She wanted to give him a normal life, but she wondered how she could do that with all this hanging over her head.

The sheriff's words in mid-sentence brought her out of her thoughts.

"I'm sorry, sheriff, I didn't catch that," she said.

"I was saying, Bonnie, that I don't mean to spook you," he said. "I don't want you to live the rest of your life paranoid. But at the same time, I want you to know the possibilities. In other words, I want you to be cautious as you and your son build a new life."

"I understand, sheriff, and I want to thank you for all you have done for us," she said. "You have gone above and beyond your job, and we appreciate that."

The sheriff suggested she take a different route for the rest of her trip and avoid the freeway. He gave her directions that took her along two-lane back roads to her destination.

He did not explain to Bonnie why, but he was concerned there might have been another vehicle following them. He did advise her to buy a hand-held GPS blocker somewhere in Lexington and start using it before leaving the city. He was certain the people Delgado was working for had been following her movements using the GPS in the truck. There was very little trust from high-level criminals in the underlings they got to do their bidding. The sheriff figured the high levels would stab anyone in the back to get their way, so they expected the same from those below them.

Having called the Hazard property caretaker when they were getting close, Bonnie and Curtis met him at the property to get the house keys he had in his possession. They then went inside, taking only what they needed for the night. They would bring in their things in the morning and begin to settle in.

Chapter 14

Bonnie watched with satisfaction as Curtis tore the wrapping from the gift she had gotten him. On the small kitchen table in front of them was a round chocolate cake with white frosting. On top was a candle in the shape of the number eight, with a whisp of smoke trailing up from it after Curtis had blown it out.

Also seated at the table were Lauralei, who had driven from Albany, and Walter Urbitkit, the Hazard property caretaker. The four had enjoyed a delicious dinner of old-fashioned roast beef with all the trimmings just more than an hour earlier. There were smiles all around, and joy filled the room. It was the level of joy Bonnie and Curtis had not felt in a long time.

A year had passed since Logan Delgado had been stabbed to death in the bedroom of the house in Albany, Wyoming, at Bonnie's and Curtis' hands. While this day was one of celebration because Curtis turned eight years old, the memory of that day was still deep in the back of both their memories. But starting their new life had helped them to push those memories back into the recesses of their minds. Festive times such as these helped push those memories deeper into the shadows.

In the seven months since Bonnie and Curtis arrived in Hazard, she had been busy stacking the building blocks of their new lives.

Within a month of arriving, Bonnie found a job as a clerk in the Sherman County courthouse in Loup City. She worked in the records office. Bonnie felt fortunate to have gotten the job, and there was a sense of pride that she had become employed so quickly. What she did not know is the person who hired her had hesitated at her lack of experience and the events she had been involved with in Wyoming. But Bonnie had included Sheriff Moore and Holly as references. Their explanation of what had transpired in Albany and their insistence that Bonnie would make an outstanding employee turned the tide.

Curtis was enrolled in school in Litchfield, a small town about eight miles northwest of Hazard and about twenty-five miles south of Loup City, with a little backtracking. Instead of riding the bus to and from school, Curtis rode to the Litchfield school with his mother when she drove to work and back. He was happy to not have to ride the bus. It allowed him to spend more time with his mother, though it was only twenty more minutes per day. Every minute with her was precious to him.

He continued to do well in school as far as his studies were concerned. His interactions with his fellow students and school staff were somewhat less than they had been in Albany. But the school counselor at the beginning of the school year attributed that to the move to a new location.

"Considering that he had trouble opening up to people in his former school, this is not unusual," Lesley Olmstead, the Litchfield Elementary School counselor, told Bonnie during a meeting after the third week of school. "He is now in a new state, new town, new school. There's always an adjustment period."

Bonnie shared with Lesley the history of why they made the move, leaving out the details of how her former husband had died. While all that would eventually have to be divulged when she applied for the job at the courthouse, she did not believe it was necessary to tell the school staff. She was concerned those details would get out and create issues for Curtis. She could deal with it if the time came for her to explain her involvement, but Curtis did not need that hanging over his head.

"He has been through a lot," Bonnie said. "I think it has affected him a great deal."

"Children are introverted for a great many reasons," Lesley said. "Some of what Curtis has been through certainly could be playing into it for him."

She paused a moment before going on.

"But another factor could be what you have gone through," she finally said. "He may be worried that anything he says about what you have endured could be harmful to you."

Bonnie nodded, feeling that pang of guilt for having killed Delgado and bringing all that upon them both.

"What can I do to help him through his adjustment?" she asked the counselor.

"Well, you've already taken the first step, getting him -- and yourself -- into a new environment," Lesley said. "I suggest you continue to build that new life for the two of you. Keep everything as positive as you can."

Bonnie took the counselor's advice to heart. In the following months, she did her best not to discuss the negative aspects of their lives in Albany. That was not an easy task if the subject came up, as since Vince's death on the rig, there seemed to be very few positive aspects to that period in their lives.

She also talked in very positive terms about their new home in Hazard. That was easier, in some respects. The small two-bedroom house was in very good shape, thanks to Walter. It was located on an acre of land in the southeast portion of town. The north and west sides of the property were bordered by other large residential lots, and the east side fronted farmland. Curtis loved watching the workers and machinery in action.

The south side faced single-line railroad tracks and Nebraska Highway 2, both running diagonally from northwest to southeast.

Across the highway was the tree-lined curvaceous Mud Creek, a portion sandwiched between Nebraska Highway 10, going north to south, and Nebraska Highway 2, the crossing of which formed a triangle at the northern edge of town. That area would eventually become a very special place for Curtis.

One part of their new home that Bonnie and Curtis both missed about their previous one was the terrain. In Wyoming, they had mountains. In Nebraska, they did not. Bonnie had never imagined she would see an area so flat. The highest point in the state is five thousand four hundred-twenty-four-foot Panorama Point at a point near where Wyoming and Nebraska butt up against each other just north of the Colorado border, a little more than three-hundred miles from Hazard. The lowest point is eight hundred-forty feet near the Missouri River. Hazard was two thousand one hundred and six feet above sea level.

In contrast, they were more than seven thousand feet in Albany, as the University of Wyoming officials boasted for their athletic teams when they played at home. The thin air made it difficult on visiting opponents, or so the myth went.

They both missed the mountains, with their snow-capped beauty a majority of the year. But standing in Hazard on a clear day, one can turn a three-hundred-sixty-degree circle and see only a small bump up north outside of Loup City.

Being such a flat area, with few natural obstructions, the wind blew hard and often in the Hazard area during the winter. And they did not get away from the snow, although there wasn't as much. Usually, Nebraska gets thirty or so inches of snowfall during a year, while more than double that was common where Bonnie and Curtis had lived in Wyoming. They experienced some cold days and nights that first winter, but again, not as cold as they were used to.

Despite the lack of mountains, Bonnie was certain she would adjust well to the new area. But she wasn't sure about Curtis. He said very little about how he felt with the move. When she saw him watch the farm work in the nearby fields with such pleasure and concentration, she had hopes he was coming out of the shell he seemed to be within. But that was the only time she saw any emotion from him regarding their new home and life.

"That boy's not right," Walter had remarked during a visit to the property to do some weatherizing after Bonnie and Curtis had lived there three months. Initially, Bonnie's motherly instincts took over her reaction.

"That's a shitty thing to say," she snapped at Walter. "He has been through a lot of trauma."

But on reflection, she understood Walter's perspective and apologized to him for her outburst the next time he was at the property. She realized that she had not shared any details of what had happened in the Albany house that fateful night. She did tell him the barest information about the incident, specifically leaving out the fact that Curtis had administered the coup de grace to his stepfather, and the further fact that he felt no remorse for his action.

"I can see why he is so introverted," Walter replied when Bonnie finished the tale. "Has he gotten any counseling?"

Curtis' teacher, Daniel, at the Albany County ESD, had tried to get the boy to talk about why he was so sullen and self-isolated. But Curtis would only respond with, "I don't know," and find a way to change the subject. Daniel had shared these attempted counseling sessions with Bonnie. His advice to her had been to broach the subject casually and listen when Curtis was ready to talk about it. But that never happened.

As time passed and she got nowhere with her attempts to get Curtis to open up, she eventually made fewer attempts. By the time of his intimate eighth birthday party, she had completely given up her efforts. But she vowed she would be ready if her son ever opened up.

The birthday party was over, and Bonnie and Lauralei were doing the dishes while Walter helped Curtis put his new gifts away in his room. It was late on a Wednesday, and the following day was a work day for Bonnie and a school day for Curtis. She wanted them both in bed soon.

"I think that went well," Lauralei said as she dried the roasting pan that had held the roast beef.

"Yes, certainly better than his seventh birthday," Bonnie answered in a hushed tone. She did not want Curtis to hear the remark and bring back those bad memories.

Lauralei glanced at her friend with her peripheral vision. She was a little surprised Bonnie would even mention that dreadful night. She was certain something like that would never leave a person's mind, at least not reasoning adults. But over time, it can be mitigated. It had taken her some time to push the visions of what she found in the house when answering her friend's call for help.

But Lauralei was concerned that her friend might still be traumatized by it.

"How are you doing?" she asked. She did not specifically refer to the incident in case Curtis could hear.

"I'm doing okay," Bonnie said. "I still remember it. But it's getting better with time. And coming here has really helped."

In contrast to the Albany house, which had an open floor plan, the kitchen in this house was a separate room off the living room. There was a doorway, with no door, and a serving window into the adjacent small dining area. That did mute their conversation somewhat from the other areas of the house, including the bedrooms, which were both on the opposite side of the structure, with Curtis' bedroom the farthest away from the kitchen. A two-car garage was off the kitchen.

Despite the muffling of conversations from other areas, Bonnie moved away from the sink and glanced up the hallway toward the far bedroom. She could hear Walter talking softly to Curtis, though she could not make out what he was saying. She returned to her task at the sink.

"I am worried about Curtis, though," she said. "He's never said a word about that night since I got out of jail, except for that one time at the Taco John's in Sidney."

"Maybe that's his way of coping with it," Lauralei offered.

Bonnie doubted that. One of the things that helped her get through it so far was her conversations with Lauralei. But his mother was the only one Curtis could talk to about the event. And Bonnie could tell he either was making an effort to keep it to himself, or he had suppressed the memories. She had read enough and seen programs on television that claimed suppressing traumatic memories was a way young children dealt with them.

But either way, Bonnie did not want to push her son to talk about the killing for fear if he did suppress the memories that her insistence he talk about it traumatize him.

Lauralei was due back at work on Friday, so she planned to head back to Wyoming first thing the next morning. So once the dishes were done, they bid Walter good night, and after he left, they all went to bed. Lauralei slept in Curtis' room and he slept with his mother.

Just as she was about to doze off for the night, Bonnie felt Curtis squeeze her hand. Lying on her right side, she opened her eyes to find Curtis looking at her with an expression of contentment she hadn't seen on the boy's face since before his own father had died.

"Thank you for bringing us here, Mom," he said. "It's like last year never happened."

Bonnie was so taken aback by the remark she had no idea what to say in return. But it was quickly clear that a response was not necessary. Curtis released her hand, wrapped his small arms around her and squeezed tightly. She tried to control her body movements and was glad to know that while they embraced, Curtis could not see the tears of joy pouring from her eyes.

Chapter 15

In the nearly three years since Bonnie and Curtis had left Wyoming, Bonnie had attended several parent-teacher conferences about her son's progress at Litchfield Elementary School. But not once had she been called to meet with the principal about her son's behavior.

In the meetings with his teachers, the reports were much the same as they had been with Daniel with the Albany County Education Service District. Curtis was an exceptional student. His work in the classroom was far above the average.

However, his teachers were all concerned about his lack of social interaction. They could not classify him as anti-social. They acknowledged that he tried to make friends, but they could see that it was difficult for him. They explained to Bonnie that it was clear to them that Curtis, now eleven years old, had difficulty trusting others. And when other students tried to talk to him, his responses were very basic - when he responded at all.

It was more than being shy, or adjustment to a new school environment, the teachers insisted.

Bonnie gave the family's history, again leaving out the specific details of Curtis' involvement in the death of his stepfather. While that helped the teachers understand a little bit more, it did not help them come up with ways to help Curtis make friends.

But when Bonnie got the call from the school requesting her presence to meet with the principal, she knew it was more than the normal meeting to discuss Curtis' problems adjusting.

"Your son injured another boy today," Timothy Bass, the Litchfield principal, told Bonnie matter-of-factly when she sat in a stiff chair across the desk from the man. He was in his mid-thirties, clean-shaven with short cropped hair, somewhat attractive, but with a stern, business-like expression.

"What happened?" Bonnie asked, trying to present the same business-like attitude as the principal but not quite succeeding.

"There was an altercation in the hallway, and the other boy's nose was broken," the principal said. "The other boy claims your son punched him without provocation."

"And what did Curtis say happened?" Bonnie asked.

"Well, he's not saying anything. I am hoping you can talk to him; maybe he will tell you," the principal said.

Neither spoke for a moment. Bonnie was considering the situation. She wondered why the principal was not telling her about the consequences Curtis would face because of his actions. She knew from her experience in the legal system in Wyoming that if a case was as cut and dried as he implied, she would be hearing about a suspension or expulsion. There was something he was holding back.

"Were there other kids around when this happened?" she asked.

"Yes, the hallway was full of people," Bass said.

"And what are they telling you?" Bonnie asked.

"Well, we haven't talked to anyone else yet; we're still trying to identify those who actually saw the incident," Bass said.

In addition to her brush with the law, Bonnie's two-and-a-half years in the Sherman County Courthouse taught her a lot about procedures in investigations. She needed to let the principal and his staff do their work in talking to potential witnesses. She also knew she had to get Curtis to open up, to her and to the principal.

Bonnie was certain the claims of no provocation in the incident were bogus. Curtis' approach to life was to keep to himself and avoid difficult situations. But remembering the incident at the Centennial school in Wyoming, she also knew that his patience with difficult people had its limits, and he was capable of striking out if he felt backed into a corner. She suspected that was the case in this incident.

"What happened today at school?" she asked Curtis when they were alone in a small teacher's workroom.

"I hurt someone," he responded timidly.

"Why did you do that?" she asked.

"I don't know," he whispered.

While Curtis had been more open with his mother in the past years since that first night in Hazard, when they were talking about difficult or uncomfortable subjects, it took some prodding to get him to speak up. But he always did eventually.

However, Bonnie felt a need to get to the bottom of this subject as quickly as possible. She wanted to keep her son on the track of improvement. She gently lifted her son's chin so they were looking at each other eye to eye.

"I think you do know, but you're scared to tell anyone," she said.

"I'm not scared," he said with a little defiance in his voice.

"So why won't you tell me what happened?" she asked. She dropped her hand from his chin and they retained the eye lock.

"Because it won't matter. I'll be in trouble," Curtis said.

"That may or may not be true, Curtis. But either way, you need to take responsibility for what you've done," his mother said.

"But he won't because I hurt him," Curtis said angrily.

"Why did you hurt him, Curtis?" Bonnie asked.

She saw his defiant resolve melting. He hung his head again.

"I didn't mean to," he said.

"Tell me what happened," his mother instructed.

It took a few moments for Curtis to gather his thoughts. He then told his mother that he had been walking down the hallway among the throng of students heading back to class after the lunch break. Amid the crowd, he brushed up against several people, all of whom gave him an annoyed look as they continued on their way. All but one.

A boy a year older and a couple inches taller than Curtis turned on him after they bumped shoulders.

"Quit touching me, you fag," the boy said.

Curtis ignored him and tried to continue on his way, but the boy grabbed his upper arm and spun him around.

"Did you hear what I said, queer boy?" the boy said menacingly.

Curtis tried to free his arm from the boy's grip but couldn't. They were just a couple feet from the wall and when Curtis made another unsuccessful attempt to get free. The boy squeezed his arm. It was painful and Curtis grimaced.

"Little gaybird can't take it," the other boy laughed, looking around for support from others around him.

It was at that moment that Curtis dropped the books in his free arm and lunged at the boy. Caught off guard, the boy turned toward the wall to try and dodge Curtis' extended arm.

Curtis took several steps forward, forcing the boy closer to the wall. The movement slammed him up against the wall, face first. Blood spattered on the wall, and the boy shrieked in pain, letting loose his grip on Curtis to cover his nose with both hands.

The hallway quickly emptied when several teachers came out of their rooms to see what the commotion was. Curtis stood a foot away from the other boy, who was still facing the bloody wall, whimpering into his hands.

Bonnie shared Curtis' version of the confrontation with the principal before taking her son home. Several days later, she was called at work and asked to see the principal when she picked up Curtis at school.

After they exchanged pleasantries, they sat down to talk. This time, Bass directed Bonnie to a leather-covered love seat and he sat on a matching easy chair placed diagonally facing the love seat. The less formal atmosphere put Bonnie at ease, which was the principal's goal.

"I have talked to all the students who were in the hallway during the incident," Bass said. "Two students corroborated Curtis' version of the events, almost to the letter."

"Almost?" Bonnie asked.

"One student said it appeared the other boy deliberately bumped into Curtis and the other mentioned one other derogatory comment the other boy made."

"And what was that?" she asked.

"It's not really important," Bass said.

"What was it?" Bonnie repeated, this time with a little more force in her voice.

Bass hesitated a few seconds before responding with a look of disgust on his face.

"He called you son a... retard, according to that student," Bass said.

Bonnie's face reddened with anger.

"And what did the rest of those kids in the hallway say happened," Bonnie asked.

Bass' face took on a look of embarrassment.

"They all said they didn't see exactly what happened so didn't want to say anything," he answered.

Bonnie's mood changed from anger to satisfaction. In her mind, Curtis was vindicated.

"So that means the other boy is going to be punished," Bonnie said, not even phrasing it as a question.

"Yes, we cannot tolerate the shaming by..." Bass began.

"Shaming?" Bonnie erupted. "Are you saying my son is all those things, but you won't allow people to point it out?" The angry red returned to her face.

Bass was taken aback. He did not expect her to react angrily to his use of the word. It was a term widely used these days for people trying to make others feel guilty or ashamed of their physical or mental states.

"No, Ms. Herden, I am not making any assumptions about your son," Bass said a little more firmly than he intended. He went on, but in a modified tone. "Maybe... actually, it was a poor choice of words."

"You bet it was," Bonnie said.

"What I'm trying to convey is we cannot tolerate any kind of hateful terms on this campus, no matter the circumstances," Bass said, trying to ignore her comment.

"So what kind of punishment is this other boy going to get?" Bonnie asked.

"I can't speak for what his parents will do, but as far as the school is concerned he will be in detention with our counselor for the next week," he explained. "She will impress upon him the need to be sensitive and tolerant toward others."

Bonnie was not totally satisfied with the response. She believed it was typical of the liberal-minded people that populated school staffs. Her parents instilled in her a sense of responsibility and accountability through tough, but not abusive, discipline. As a young child, she was no stranger to a good spanking when it was deserved, or a stern lecture if that was the best course of action.

However, the school philosophy had moved away from corporal punishment -- the wooden paddle was a thing of the past. Now it was about counseling, talking things out. Sensitivity training was now the going trend.

But Bonnie figured detention was the best she was going to get for Curtis' tormentor. She began to rise to leave the principal's office. But his next words stopped her in mid-stand.

"At the same time, Ms. Herden, we cannot condone Curtis' reaction to the insults," he said. "Violence, especially on campus, has to be dealt with."

Bonnie slowly finished standing.

"And what does that mean for Curtis?" she asked.

"There is usually about thirty minutes between the final bell and when you arrive to pick him up," Bass said, remaining seated. "In that time, I will talk with Curtis about some techniques he can use to curb his impulsive reaction to uncomfortable things."

Bonnie was somewhat placated by that solution, although still not happy that her son was seen as having done something wrong for, in her mind, simply trying to put a stop to bullying.

She did agree that violence was not the answer. But she believed her son when he said he did not intend to hurt the other boy. She also believed he had a right to defend himself.

She left the principal's office without another word.

In the next month, things were peaceful for Curtis. The other boy, Gerald "Gerry" Kline, kept his distance from Curtis during the school day. He was resentful at having to be in detention and be lectured about his behavior. But he knew that another confrontation so soon after this one would surely get him suspended from school. That would not sit well with his parents.

But as time went by, his resentment continued to build, and he blamed Curtis for his predicament. As most bullies do, he spent much of his time plotting revenge.

Getting that was going to be a bit difficult, as Gerry lived in Littlefield, almost eight miles from Hazard. Since he was only twelve, Gerry did not yet drive, and walking that distance was not in his nature. The only time they would be in close proximity would be at school, and taking action there was not feasible -- at least in the near future.

But Gerry was determined to get what he believed was his deserved vengeance.

Curtis knew nothing of Gerry's intentions. But he was not so naive as to think there would not be some repercussions from the incident. In that first week, he was extra cautious while at the school. But when Gerry kept away from him, he began to slowly lower his guard.

In addition, he was enjoying his time at school. In the months since they moved to Hazard, Curtis was slow to make friends, mostly because of his own emotional isolation. But after hearing from his mother that two students had stood up for him over the incident in the school hallway, he began to let down his emotional defenses just a little. His mother did not know the names of the two who had backed up his story, so Curtis could not approach them.

However, several students began saying hello to him as they passed in the hallways at school. Eventually, those hellos turned into short chit-chats.

But once that initial month was over, so was Curtis' honeymoon.

Chapter 16

Gerry Kline was the middle child in a large household. He had two older sisters and three younger brothers. Both his parents had to hold down two jobs to keep the bill collectors away and make sure there was enough food to feed all the mouths.

His father, Hank, was a farm hand during the day and did mechanical repair at his home or at the owner's property for several farmers in the area during his off hours. The mother, Irene, waited tables at a Litchfield cafe and had a part-time job at a hardware store during the mornings.

Because much of their time was spent trying to bring in enough revenue to support the family, there was little time left over to spend with the children. They were left to fend for themselves much of the time. Both the older girls were in high school and were forced to be responsible for preparing the majority of the family meals, doing the housework and shepherding the younger children. That left them no time for social or extra-curricular activities or events at school. While they met their household responsibilities with flying colors, they resented the fact they could not spend time with their friends or be involved in activities.

The girls would be out of school in a few years, and they longed for the opportunity to leave their family responsibilities behind. When they were gone, those responsibilities would fall on Gerry, as the next oldest. His sisters knew he was not up to the task. But they were so focused on their plans to shed the yoke of the family burdens, they did not care. That was going to be their parents' problem.

For some, especially girls, in the small Nebraska towns in Sherman County, getting away and seeing the wider world was their top priority.

Most boys had a different outlook. They saw themselves as following in their fathers' footsteps as farmers or other occupations related to farming. Gerry was in this category.

He also believed the only way he could achieve that life goal was to be tough and hard. But there is a difference between that approach and being so tough and hard that one becomes a bully. Gerry was in that latter category as well.

Gerry believed that boys who were quiet and non-aggressive were weak. He believed only the strong survive and the weak suffer. And if he had to help the weak suffer, so be it.

That was not necessarily an attitude he learned from his father. Hank had a very healthy work ethic and a strong sense of responsibility. As his family grew larger and the need for more income became necessary, Hank's attention to passing those attributes along to his children faded. He believed he was teaching them by example rather than through his words. But with all the working hours, those words, that could have re-enforced his actions, were absent.

His political views and outlook on life tended to the conservative side. So when he did speak in front of the children, those views impressed themselves upon them. Gerry, for one, took them to heart, and took them to another level.

Anyone who deviated from the outdated traditional roles of American society was considered weak and even abnormal by Gerry. He hated the homosexual lifestyle, seeing it as a choice. Even those who did not approve of the lifestyle but condoned it he considered a part of it.

He believed a woman's place in a family setting was as a homemaker. While he understood the need for his parents to earn additional income to support their family, he still resented his mother for working outside the home. He believed his father should carry a heavier load to allow his mother to fulfill the role he was determined should be hers.

Gerry was also a budding white supremacist. There were very few blacks in the rural areas of Nebraska, but Native Americans were plentiful. He looked at both races as inferior.

These were the views and attitudes that fueled Gerry's campaign to get revenge on Curtis Herden for the predicament Gerry found himself in during his period of detention.

While Curtis' nemesis, Gerry Kline, had already established the personality he would have for the rest of his life, Curtis was just beginning to redefine himself. Up until the incident in the school hallway, he had been quiet, sullen, introverted and angry. Much of the cause for those traits could be traced back to the death of his father, which he barely remembered but suffered by his absence in his life. That was compounded by the strong and varied emotions stemming from his stepfather's death, the memories of which were burned into his brain.

But since the hallway incident and its aftermath, things began to change. He was pleased that Gerry was punished, even though Curtis thought he got off easy compared to the way the other boy treated him and the things he called him.

Curtis was also gratified with the time he spent daily with the principal, though at first, he viewed it as a punishment he believed he did not deserve. But, Timothy Bass was respectful to him and provided some helpful tips on how to control his reactions to upsetting events.

Other students saw the subtle changes in Curtis and began to cautiously open up to him. He made several new friends in the weeks following the incident with Gerry, and he found he felt more comfortable talking to others.

The friends he made were a diverse group, including two Native Americans, two whites, the one African American at the school and one Asian. Two of that group of friends were girls. This circle of friends was drawn to Curtis because they all had something in common -- they were also bullied by Gerry and his gang of friends at one time or another.

Curtis had always been the type of kid who did not categorize people, as was so common among young and old alike. In terms of ethnicity, he was color blind.

Regarding sexual preferences, he knew little about it. While in Wyoming, he had heard about an incident in which a university student, who was openly gay, was taken by a group of other students into the fields outside of Laramie and beaten severely because of his lifestyle, tied to a fence and left to die.

When he heard about that incident, as it was the main topic of discussion at his school for several weeks thereafter, he thought it cruel that a group of people would gang up on a single person. The reasons for it were also confusing to him. He asked his mother to explain it.

"Well, you know how a man and woman fall in love and get married, and eventually they have sex and make children," Bonnie had told him. She had explained to him, after being questioned a year earlier, in very basic terms what sex was.

"Yes, I remember what you said," he answered, wondering what that had to do with the event he had heard about.

"This boy that was beaten up and tied to a fence, he wasn't like normal boys," Bonnie said. "He liked to be with other boys."

"I like to be with other boys. Does that mean some people will beat me up?" Curtis asked, puzzled.

"I don't mean he liked being with boys the way you do, to play cars or cowboys and Indians with," Bonnie said, struggling to find the right words for someone as young as Curtis. "I mean, like a man and a woman would when they get married."

Curtis cocked his head and thought that over for a moment.

"You mean they would put their wieners in each other?" he asked.

Bonnie had to stifle a giggle.

"But how would they do that? Boys don't have..." he began, then made a face like he had just found a turd in his cereal, as he put two and two together. "In their butts? That's gross!"

This time, Bonnie couldn't stop the giggle from trickling out.

"Yes, it is," she finally said when she was able to control herself.

"I don't think I'd like that," Curtis said.

And that remained his attitude about homosexuality, although he never developed the kind of hatred toward gay people as some others did. Not that he was exposed to it much. After the death of the university student, gay people kept quiet about it in Albany County, and the same must have been true in Sherman County in Nebraska, as Curtis had never heard of any in the short time they had been in Hazard. Gerry's accusations in the school hallway were the first references he had heard there.

Gerry's abstinence from his campaign of vengeance toward Curtis began to change, but very subtly, a little more than a month after his detention began. Because his attitude wasn't changing, the detention continued. But after two months, the counselor threw up her hands and told Principal Bass there was nothing more she could do.

But Gerry, like most bullies, was a grudge holder. He wanted Curtis to suffer for forcing him to be kept after school and lectured. It did not help that a fair share of what little time his parents had to spend with him and their other children was spent talking to all the children about treating people fairly and politely.

Hank and Irene were hard-working and decent people, and they wanted to impart those qualities on their children. However, the financial dynamics of the family made it difficult for them to spend the kind of time they needed to impress upon their children their belief that people were the same, no matter their ethnicity, gender and even sexual philosophy.

Despite their mostly conservative outlook, the adult Klines believed a person's sexual preference was something they were born with and that there was nothing wrong with that. They had expressed this outlook in front of the children several times. But Gerry, having gotten a different viewpoint from his grandparents on both sides of the family, could not bring himself to agree with his parents. He resented his parents for their beliefs, and that resentment festered and fueled a defiance that grew with each passing day. His parents' sharing of their views about the treatment of people following Gerry's encounter with Curtis was like pouring lighter fluid on a campfire.

Gerry's desire to get back at Curtis was also stoked by the fact that the younger boy got the best of him. Among his cadre of friends, Gerry took some ribbing for having gotten his nose bloodied by the "faggot." His arguments that Curtis caught him by surprise, and that was the only reason he got slammed against the wall did little to stop the little jabs.

He was determined to turn the tables.

His renewed campaign against the new kid started with angry looks when they passed in the halls of the school. Curtis took no notice of them at first. But when one of his friends pointed them out, he did his best just to look away whenever he noticed Gerry in the vicinity. At other times, he practiced some of the techniques Bass had taught him. Curtis was developing patience.

Gerry's campaign escalated by small degrees -- moving in such a way that it was impossible for Curtis to avoid seeing his stares, deliberately bumping him in the hallway as they passed, and eventually starting the name-calling again. This went on for the next couple of years.

But during the summers, Curtis got a respite since he and Gerry lived in different towns. It was during those summers that Curtis was able to truly enjoy his time in the new home in Hazard. Bonnie left him alone at home during those summers while she went to work in Loup City. Walter made it a point to be at the house from time to time each day that Bonnie was away to make sure Curtis was doing okay and staying out of trouble.

The latter was not a real big chore, since Curtis was well-mannered and he hung around with no one because his small group of friends all lived in Litchfield or Loup City and, like him, had no means of motorized transportation. It was a bit far for any of them to ride their bicycles to see each other.

But Curtis did not mind. In fact, he enjoyed the times that Walter was at the house. Most of his visits were to do landscape maintenance on the property. Curtis tagged along, watching carefully and asking a multitude of questions about the work. He was also just as curious when Walter did maintenance on the house.

He also asked many questions about the farming industry in general and the farms around Hazard in particular. As he soaked in the knowledge, Curtis began to believe that farming was to be his goal when he was old enough.

Walter helped him get lawn mowing jobs during the summer and after school. He lent him his landscape equipment as needed until, when he turned thirteen, he had saved enough to buy his own lawn mower.

But Curtis had bigger plans. When he turned fourteen, he would be old enough to get an actual job, and he set his sights on working for one of the farmers in the area. For the time being, he learned more about the business.

However, the summer after his thirteenth birthday, something happened that changed the direction of Curtis' life in ways that he could never have imagined.

Chapter 17

The period between his seventh and eighth-grade years became known to Curtis as the summer of Mary.

Ruth Marie Jung and her parents emigrated from Germany to the United States when she was two years old. They began their new lives in the U.S. In the state of Ohio, where her father, Joachim, worked in a steel mill. But when he was laid off, he took jobs where he could, mostly at farms. Her mother, Ava, began waiting tables when her husband was laid off.

Joachim's work in the fields and his ability to fix just about anything mechanical gave him a reputation that began to spread. When a Hazard area large farm owner was in Ohio to buy some equipment at a farm auction, he heard of Jung and sought him out. It didn't take him long to decide he wanted this man working on his farm. He made Joachim, as the famous movie line goes, an offer he could not refuse, and the family, three members of which had gotten their U.S. Citizenship two years earlier, moved to Hazard in the middle of July.

The Jungs rented a house in the north area of the small community and settled in. Joachim's goal was to save enough to buy a piece of land and then build his own home on it.

Curtis first laid eyes on Ruth Jung from a distance one day while he was in the backyard of his and his mother's home, watching the irrigation standards rotating around the circular field just to the east. He happened to glance to his right and saw her at the end of the street, walking toward their property.

He found that he could not look back toward the field. His vision was locked on this girl, for what reason he could not understand at the moment. What he did know was that his throat began to get dry, and it felt like someone had stepped on the accelerator for his heart.

As she got closer, he could make out more detail. She was wearing Jean cutoff shorts, riding high enough that it made her shapely legs look longer than they actually were. She also had on a gray T-shirt that fit fairly tight, revealing two distinct shapes on her chest. She had a thin waist, but not so thin as to make her hips appear overly large.

She was nearly to the property line when he could make out the details of her face. As she swiveled her head from side to side every so often to study the neighborhood, her long, blond, straight hair flipped back to reveal a slightly egg-shaped face with shallow cheekbones, a button nose and a smallish mouth. Her eyes were inquisitive, although at a distance between them Curtis could not distinguish their color.

Not that Curtis was focusing on her eyes.

When she reached the south line of the Herden property, she raised her right arm and waved casually, but she didn't break stride. Her mouth curled upward at the corners into a broad smile, or as broad as that small mouth could muster.

As she passed, Curtis watched her hips pop up and down, moving her round, full butt cheeks in a hypnotic rhythm.

Curtis timidly waved in return, and suddenly felt a tightness in the crotch of his Jeans he had never felt before.

Walter came to the Herden house two days later and found Curtis again watching the activity in the field to the east. However, as he approached the boy, he could tell his attention was not fully on the field.

"Not much to see out there today," Walter said as he appeared at Curtis' left side. The boy reacted ever so slightly, having not heard the older man coming since he was so deep in his daydream, replaying the walk of the mystery girl up the street.

"There might be in a couple of days," Curtis replied, without looking at Walter.

In the six-plus years he and his mother had lived in Hazard, he watched carefully the cycle of planting and harvesting the fields of hay grass. Normally, the first cutting took place around the third week of June, with a second cutting, with less yield, done about a month later.

The field Curtis had been carefully watching, in between school and his lawn mowing jobs, had been harvested a week earlier in June than usual this year. The second cutting should have been going on now, but the farmer was letting it go a little longer, trying to get as much out of a second cutting as possible, Curtis guessed.

They both stood in silence for a few seconds, watching the thigh-high hay waving lazily in the light, warm breeze.

"I've been asked to mow a yard and trim some edges and bushes at a house on the north end of town. But I'm all booked up for today," Walter said. "It's a job you can handle if you want it."

Curtis readily accepted. Walter handed him a slip of paper with an address written on it.

"Use your mower, and I left a pair of hedge trimmers and a weed whacker on the porch," Walter said, pointing to the house. "I've got an appointment I'm already late for, or I'd take you up there."

"That's okay, I can walk it," Curtis said already heading for the house to gather his gear.

When he got to the address, he found a property about the size of his own and a similar-looking house. Pushing the mower with the weed whacker and trimmers tied to the handle with rope to near the front door. He walked up onto the porch, pulled the screen door open and knocked lightly on the main door.

When the door opened, he suddenly felt the same racing heart and tightening in his crotch he felt two days ago. There was no mistaking who was standing facing him -- the girl from the street. She was dressed similarly, only this time, her shirt was light blue.

Curtis felt his face heat up as the rush of blood-colored his cheeks a bright crimson. He tried to speak but for the life of him could not find any words.

"Hello," the girl said sweetly, with that same smile that was etched into Curtis' mind.

"Uh, hello," Curtis finally managed, but his throat was so dry it sounded more like the croak of a bullfrog. He swallowed what little spit he had on his tongue and tried again.

"Walter Urbitkit was supposed to do your lawn, but he had an appointment, so he sent me," Curtis said, his voice a little more normal but getting rougher toward the end of the lengthy sentence.

"You seem a bit young to be a landscaper," the girl said. Her voice was as smooth as velvet and as light as the air, or so it seemed to Curtis. The way in which she spoke the words sounded like she could be teasing him a little.

Curtis also noticed an odd way she pronounced the R at the end, almost as if she rolled it off her tongue like a barrel.

"Walter has been teaching me," Curtis said sheepishly.

"Oh, so you are his apprentice," she said.

"I guess," he replied, looking down at her petite bare feet. He saw the nails were painted bright yellow. She had her hands behind her back, so he couldn't tell if her fingernails were also painted.

"I should get started," Curtis said and slowly turned and left the porch without another word.

"I'll be here if you need anything," the girl said.

Curtis did not hear the door shut. He glanced back over his shoulder and saw her still standing in the doorway, watching him. He quickly turned his head forward, lest she think he was staring at her.

Mowing the lawn took Curtis nearly two hours. Since there were no gas stations in Hazard, his mother had helped him pick out a good-quality electric mower and a fifty-foot utility cord. He only had to stop twice to move the cord to different outdoor outlets.

He had just finished the mowing and was wrapping the cord around the handle in the front yard when he felt a gentle tap on his shoulder. He turned to find the girl standing behind him. He was tired and sweaty, so the hormone excitement that he felt earlier wasn't present this time.

"You've been working hard. Do you want to take a rest?" she asked as she pointed to the front porch. Curtis saw a small table and two chairs set up in the corner closest to them. On it were a pitcher and two tall glasses.

"It won't take me long to finish, then I need to get home," he said shyly, even though he really wanted to accept.

"Oh, c'mon, just a few minutes," the girl said. "I have something cold for you to drink."

She took his hand and stepped toward the house. He did not move, but he did not let go of her hand. It was slightly smaller than his. Her skin felt smooth as silk, and he felt as if he were fouling her with his sweaty palms. But he did not want to let go.

"C'mon," she said, tagging his arm gently. He complied.

She did not release his hand until they were seated at the wicker table. He could not help but notice that she did not wipe his sweat from her hand. He, however, swiped his hands on his jeans as covertly as he could. He also noticed that her fingernails were painted a light blue with what appeared to Curtis tiny specks of slivery glitter.

"I apologize for my manners," she said as she poured him a glass of lemonade. "My name is Ruth. But please call me Mary."

"I'm Curtis," he said.

"Have you lived here long?" she asked, pushing a saucer of cookies toward him. He took one.

"We moved here six years ago, when I was seven," he said.

"Really, then you are thirteen, like me," Mary said.

Curtis nodded, taking a bite of the cookie. He could taste peanut butter, but he also crunched on something as he chewed. Mary noticed the puzzled look on his face.

"Don't you like them?" she asked.

"Yes, I love peanut butter cookies, one of my favorites," he responded. "But there's something in them."

She giggled a little.

"I use chunky peanut butter instead of creamy," she said. "I think it makes them better."

"I like them," he said, taking another bite.

"So, where did you move here from?" she asked.

"Wyoming," he answered, and took a gulp of lemonade.

"That's where Yellowstone Park is, right?" she asked. Curtis nodded. "Have you ever been there?" she continued. He shook his head.

They were silent for a while as he finished his cookie. He felt like he should say something, but could not think of what more to say. He was surprised he had said as much as he had. Mary was so accepting, however, that he felt somewhat at ease with her, something else that surprised him.

Curtis could tell she wanted to talk more. He frantically searched his mind for something to say to break the silence since it seemed she was waiting for him to be more a part of the conversation. Finally, the simplest thing popped into his fuzzy mind.

"Where did you come from?" he asked.

"We moved her from Ohio. But I was born in Regensburg," she said.

"In Ohio?" he asked.

"No, Regensburg is in Germany," she said.

Curtis was suddenly intrigued. He had never met anyone from another country before. For that matter, he didn't think he had met anyone from outside of Wyoming until moving to Hazard.

"That's awesome," he heard himself exclaim. But nothing else came to mind to say. They sat in silence again for a few moments. It was beginning to get awkward until something else came to him.

"If your name is Ruth, why do you want me to call you Mary?" he asked.

She blushed a little before responding.

"My middle name is Marie. My grandmother - my father's mother - prefers I go by that name, and when she says it, it sounds more like Mary, so that's what everyone in my family has called me," she explained.

"Why does your grandmother like Marie more than Ruth?" he asked.

Mary blushed a little deeper this time, and took a few moments to gather her thoughts.

"Her father was an officer in the SS during the last world war and hated Jews," Mary said. "Ruth is a common Hebrew name."

Through his studies in school, Curtis had a basic knowledge of World War II and the Nazi regime and its hardliners' racial philosophy. However, because of his view that people are just people, he did not understand how anyone could hate another group of people because of their nationality or religion.

"I like both names," Curtis said. "But I'll call you Mary because that's what you want."

The smile returned to her face.

Again, silence reigned between them momentarily.

"I saw you the other day," Mary finally said.

Curtis simply nodded. The memories of that day came flooding back, and he replayed her walk up the street in his mind. Looking back on it and seeing her sitting across from him now, he decided his original observations were a little off. For starters, her hair was a lighter blond than he remembered; even sitting there in the shade of the porch, he could see the difference. He also now noticed she had hazel eyes, although he would call them green.

He remembered, too, their walk from the yard to the porch. He knew that he was five feet six inches tall. She appeared to be four inches shorter than he. Looking her over sitting at the table, he saw that her lips were a little fuller than he recalled, but not overly so. He let his eyes drop and saw that her breasts were a little smaller than he remembered, but still large enough at her age to leave an impression.

Suddenly, he caught himself staring at her chest, and the tightness in his jeans and the increased heart rate returned. He jerked his head up and looked out into the yard.

"I better finish and get home," he said as he stood up and quickly left the porch.

"Curtis, what's wrong?" she asked.

"I... I was rude, and I need to get my work done," he said without turning around.

As he trimmed the bushes and edged the lawn along the short walkway leading to the front door and along the fences, he saw that Mary remained seated at the table, watching him as he worked.

He completed the work in less than an hour and tied the remaining equipment to the lawn mower. He began to walk out of the yard.

"Will I see you later?" she asked from the porch.

Curtis waved without turning around but said nothing as he left the yard.

Chapter 18

Curtis stewed for the rest of the day over his meeting with Mary. He was embarrassed for staring at her tits, and he would be even more embarrassed if he had been caught at it. And how could she have not caught him? They were sitting less than three feet apart.

But she said nothing about it, and even asked about seeing him again. He was also angry at himself for not responding when she made that query. He wanted to see her again. She seemed very nice, and she had initiated a conversation with him. She seemed to have a way of getting him to respond. He had not opened up like he had with Mary to anyone except his small group of bullied friends and, of course, his mother.

Curtis could not imagine Mary fitting into the same category as his small group of friends. Who would bully such a sweet, beautiful girl?

And then there was the physical reaction he had - not once but twice.

He had always been smart for his age. He knew the biology of sexual attraction. His mother had given him the basics years ago, and that stoked his curiosity, so he read as much as he could on the subject. He knew that when boys went through adolescence, their hormones changed, and would remain that way for much of the rest of their lives.

Curtis had read about how sexual arousal caused more blood to be pumped to the male penis to make it hard. But he had never actually experienced a hard-on until he saw Mary for the first time a few days ago. He got another one when he was staring at her breasts.

But he was confused at why that would happen upon seeing a pretty girl for the first time. There was no emotional attachment between them; there had been no time for any to develop.

He wanted to talk to someone about it. Even though he and Walter had built a rapport, Curtis was not comfortable talking to him about this. He knew he might be the best chose, being a man and all. But it just didn't feel right to talk to him yet about something this personal.

That left his mother.

After dinner that evening, he timidly told Bonnie he wanted to talk about something very personal. She was a little concerned. He had said nothing about Gerry's renewed campaign of bullying in the recent past, but she knew that was a strong possibility. The fact that the principal had not called her to discuss anything put her mind a bit at ease on that score.

"What is it, Curtis," she said. "You know you can talk to me about anything."

"I met a girl the other day," he said. "And I saw her again today."

Bonnie braced herself. She knew this day would come, and in some ways, she dreaded it, but in others, she was looking forward to it. Maybe her son getting interested in girls might help him come out of his shell. It might also help him put his awful memories about the death of his father and the killing of his stepfather out of his mind. That way, he could get on with his life normally.

"And..." Bonnie urged.

"Well, when I first saw her, my thing...you know," he said, pointing at his crotch. "It got hard."

Bonnie sighed. "I'm going to have to explain all this again," she thought.

"Do you remember when I told you how men and women have sex?" she asked. "Well, when a man gets aroused..."

"Mom, I know how all that works," Curtis said. "I just don't understand why it would happen all of a sudden, and with someone I don't even know."

"It's a natural thing, Curtis," Bonnie said. "When a boy's hormones change, it could happen unexpectedly, and not just by meeting someone. You could see a picture or think of sex, and it happens."

"It happened again today," he said. "We were having lemonade at her house, and I was looking at her, you know..." He placed his cupped hands in front of his chest.

"Well, that's natural, too. Unless you were staring," Bonnie said as encouragingly as she could.

"I was staring, and I was embarrassed about it," he said angrily, but more directed toward himself rather than his mother.

"Will you be seeing her again?" Bonnie asked.

"She asked if we'd see each other later, but I was too embarrassed to answer," he said.

Bonnie reached out and took her son's hands in hers.

"Then you should go over to her house and apologize and explain to her that you were embarrassed about it," Bonnie advised.

"But what if she thinks I'm a pervert or something and doesn't want to see me again?" he said.

"She asked you about getting together again," she said. "Trust me, Curtis, she wouldn't have asked that if she didn't want to see you again."

They hugged, and she sent him to rinse the dinner dishes and put them in the dishwasher. She was delighted that it appeared someone else was showing interest in her son. Curtis had talked about his small circle of friends, but Bonnie hoped that Curtis would make more friends in their new location as he grew older. She believed it would help his social development and interactions.

But at the same time, her motherly instincts had her concerned. She knew next to nothing about this girl. Was she older or younger? Because of Curtis' mention of staring at her boobs, Bonnie guessed she was older. But by how much? And what was her interest in her son? Bonnie loved Curtis very much, but she was realistic enough to know that his social awkwardness put him at a disadvantage in making friends - and it would be even worse when it came to romantic attractions.

She did not want to press her son on the point. His self-confidence was low enough already. But she needed to find out more about this girl as subtly as possible.

The following day Curtis had three yards to mow, so he was busy much of the day. Twice as he worked, he noticed Mary walk by. She smiled and waved at him, and he timidly responded.

Curtis was still uncertain how he wanted to deal with Mary to make amends for his behavior the day before. He was uncomfortable with a direct approach of going to her home and initiating a conversation. When he was younger, he rarely spoke to people at all, and only when they asked him questions. Even then, he responded only when pressed.

Now that he had made some friends at school, he was a little more communicative with them. But even now, he usually only spoke in answer to their questions. He did not initiate conversations, nor join in unless he was invited with a question or some prodding.

He thought about writing her a note and leaving it, under cover of darkness, inside the screen door at her family's house. But he dismissed that as being somewhat cowardly. Besides, what if someone else opened and read the note?

No matter how it was done, Curtis wanted to take his mother's advice and apologize for his behavior.

One thing that kept him from settling on a method and acting upon it was the fear that Mary would reject the apology and never want to see him again. That he did not want. No matter what kind of relationship they had - good friends or just acquaintances - he wanted this girl to look upon him favorably. There was something about the way she accepted him openly and without reservation that drew him to her.

Even though his teenage emotions made him believe she was attracted to him and him alone, he was not so naïve as to not consider the possibility that her friendliness and openness were just a part of her personality.

When he completed his final yard, Curtis went home and took a quick shower to wash off the dirt and sweat. He put on a Wyoming Cowboys football T-shirt his mother had purchased for him for his latest birthday, a pair of cargo shorts and his tennis shoes without socks and took his normal station at the east-facing fence to watch the activity in the field.

On the opposite side of the circular hay field, he could see the red Farmall tractor hitched to the sickle bar mower with the hay bailer parked nearby. No one was near the equipment, so that meant the cutting would most likely start the next morning.

He stood there leaning against the fence for several minutes, lost in his thoughts about how to approach Mary. Suddenly, he felt a tap on his shoulder. He turned, expecting to see either his mother or Walter, even though he had not heard any vehicles drive onto the property.

Instead, he came face to face with Mary.

He took her in from head to toe, making sure not to rest his eyes in any one area for more than one second. But in that quick inspection, he saw that she was again wearing jean cutoffs, this time faded in color, and a navy blue blouse that fit a little baggy, but with the shirttails tied in front so that her belly button was exposed. Her blond hair, looking closer to strawberry blond this time with the sun making its slow trek to the horizon, was parted in the middle and worn down, with portions on each side of her face hanging down in front and the rest down her back. The front strands extended below her breasts, mostly covering them.

"Hello, Curtis," she cooed.

"Hi," he replied without considering his response. Thinking that was a little lame, he tried again. "Um, you look nice." He mentally kicked himself because that seemed even more lame.

"Thank you," Mary said sincerely.

They stood in silence for a moment, Curtis glancing from side to side with his eyes but keeping his face pointed straight at her. Mary kept her eyes locked on him.

"Did I do something wrong yesterday?" Mary finally asked. "You seemed to want to get away from me."

Curtis swallowed the lump that had formed in his throat. His nervousness was obvious; he was certain. That made him even more nervous. He hung his head.

"It wasn't anything you did," he muttered. "It was me. I was rude."

She reached out and with her delicate fingers and used them to lift his chin until they were looking eye to eye again.

"How were you rude?" she asked.

Curtis shuffled from foot to foot. He opened his mouth to speak, but no words came out. Mary was patient, not wanting to rush him. Finally, he believed he knew what to say.

"I was, um, staring at your...at your..." he stammered.

"My what, Curtis?" Mary prompted.

He ventured a quick glance at her chest but didn't say anything.

"What are they, Curtis," she prodded.

"Your boobs," he said quickly. "And I'm sorry for doing that. It was wrong."

"You're not the only one who has ever done that," she said, letting her hand drop from his chin. "I'm used to it."

"Doesn't it bother you?" Curtis asked.

"Well, it depends on the guy and how long they stare," she said. "I've gotten used to it because I've developed quicker than other girls my age."

"I'm sorry for doing that," was all he could think of to say.

"Curtis, stop apologizing," she said calmly. "That fact that you have tells me you're not the kind of guy who looks at a girl and only thinks about sex."

Remembering his two hard-ons in his previous encounters, he wasn't so sure she was correct in her assessment. But then he realized it had not happened this time, even when she mentioned the word "sex."

"Can we sit down and talk?" Mary asked.

Curtis cursed himself in his mind for not having the manners to offer that himself.

"Sure," he said and turned toward the house. He felt Mary take his hand in hers, and he suddenly felt his crotch start to get hard. As they walked the short distance, he thought about the coming hay cutting, his yard work, the weather - anything to soften his newfound manhood.

Sitting in two of the four wooden lawn chairs facing each other across a small fire pit, Mary looked around the property, taking it all in before she spoke first.

"This is a nice place," she said. "It's kind of like ours."

"My grandparents left it to my mom," Curtis volunteered.

"Are they dead?" she asked.

"Yes, before I was born," he answered, offering no other details. Mary was dying to know more, but she felt it might seem to Curtis that she was prying into personal matters he didn't want to talk about.

"Do you have any brothers and sisters?' she asked.

"No, it's just me and mom," he said.

"Where's your dad?" she asked.

"He's dead," Curtis said. "In a drilling accident when I was about two."

Mary suddenly felt sorry for Curtis and wanted to go to him and offer comfort. But the matter-of-fact way he had delivered those pieces of news made her hesitate.

"I'm sorry," she whispered.

"It's okay, it was a long time ago," Curtis said.

There was a long pause as they both searched for their next subject to talk about. Mary wanted to know more about him and his family, but after the most recent revelations, she was not sure how to proceed. She did not want the conversation to take a negative track.

For his part, Curtis had reverted back to his habit of waiting to be asked a question before speaking.

Finally, Mary broke the silence.

"Curtis, I would like us to be friends," she said. She could see the relief fill his face.

"I'd like that," he croaked through a suddenly dry throat. She smiled, and that made Curtis relax a little. He was about to ask her a question when they both heard a vehicle pull into the property. Bonnie's pickup came to rest on the other side of the house and Curtis glanced at his wristwatch - his father's that his mother had given him three years ago. It was nearly six-thirty in the evening.

Bonnie came around the back of the truck carrying several bulging plastic grocery bags. She set them on the porch. When she saw Curtis and Mary sitting in the lawn chairs, she continued toward them. Both the youngsters stood up.

"Hi, Mom," Curtis said.

"Hi, Baby," she said, then glanced at Mary. "I see you have company."

"This is Mary," Curtis said, blushing slightly. "Her family just moved here."

Bonnie stuck out her hand, and Mary reciprocated, and they shook.

"Nice to meet you," Mary said. She would have added Ms. and Bonnie's last name, but she and Curtis had not yet shared their last names.

"Likewise," Bonnie said. She glanced Curtis' way and nodded toward the porch. He ran over, grabbed the grocery bags and went inside the house.

"Have you had dinner yet?" Bonnie asked.

"No, ma'am," Mary answered.

"My name is Bonnie Herden," she said. "But please, call me Bonnie."

Bonnie took her cell phone out of her pocket and handed it to Mary.

"Call your parents and see if it is okay if you have dinner with us," Bonnie said. "If you'd like to," she added.

"I'd like that very much," Mary said, then started punching in numbers. "Thank you."

Chapter 19

Bonnie and Mary got along well, which pleased Curtis very much. Bonnie was gratified to learn that Mary was the same age as Curtis. She had been concerned, based on her earlier conversation with her son, that the girl might be much older, and that made her worried that Curtis could be led down roads he was not prepared for. That still could have been possible with a girl the same age, especially one as physically developed as Mary.

But after getting a chance to talk to Mary at that initial dinner at the Herden home, Bonnie's mind was put at ease. Mary seemed to be a very polite, sincere, normal girl of thirteen. Bonnie even learned, without questioning or prodding, that Mary was a bit resentful about her shapeliness because of the sexual attention it brought upon her from other boys.

Eventually, mother and son met Mary's parents. While Joachim and Ava were glad to have made some friends in their new community, their work schedules made it difficult to spend time with others. But the families were able to get together occasionally.

Curtis and Bonnie learned the Jungs had another child, a son six years older than Mary. The previous year, he had returned to Germany to enlist in that country's navy. He was assigned to a frigate, Germany's largest class of surface warships. Erich did not want U.S. Citizenship, but had celebrated the rest of his family's choice.

In the weeks before school began in mid-August, Curtis and Mary spent a lot of time together when he was not busy with yard jobs. The final weekend before they both headed back for their last year in middle school, Curtis felt comfortable enough with Mary that he wanted to share something -- something very dear to him.

"I have a special place I like to go," he told her one afternoon. "Would you like to see it?"

"Yes, Curtis, I would very much," she said.

From his house, they walked across the railroad tracks and Nebraska Highway 2. They skirted past a fenced sewage pond and along the edge of a grove of trees. Crossing a field, they came to a line of trees next to a body of water running north to south.

"This is the river. I come here to think sometimes," He told her.

Mary looked at the running water in front of her. It was not very swift. Looking right and left, Mary saw that both banks were tree-lined, except for a small portion on the opposite side several yards away.

Actually, it was not a river at all. It was called Mud Creek, and it was shallow and narrow enough that a person could wade across fairly easily, at least at the spot where they stood.

"What do you think about when you are here?" Mary asked.

"Different things," Curtis said after a moment's hesitation. "Mostly about what the world would be like without people hating each other."

Mary felt in that moment like she had found a kindred spirit. They spent more than two hours walking along the banks of the creek, sharing their thoughts about a wide range of topics. They found that they differed on a few things, but for the most part, they shared the same outlook on a number of aspects of life.

School began much as it had most years in Curtis' life. He threw himself into the work required, and he continued to score higher than his classmates. He thought nothing of it. He knew no other path than to gather in all he could and share that in his homework, quizzes and tests.

Socially, it was also similar to other years, except now he had a small circle of friends. He had hoped Mary would be a part of that group, and in the first month, she was. But she was so personable that she began making more of her own friends, students that, unknown to her in the beginning, looked upon

Curtis as a geek, an anomaly, even an outcast. As she made more friends, she spent less time with Curtis outside of class during the school days.

He did not begrudge her the fact that she was making other friends. He was disappointed, though, that those gravitating toward her would not even give him the time of day, except when they were in Mary's presence. Their two-faced approach kept Mary from discovering the truth of how they viewed Curtis for some time.

Because she was pretty and more physically developed than the other girls, Mary attracted the attention of a lot of the boys. They fawned over her and hit on her at nearly every turn. She took it in stride -- at least on the outside -- and tried to be polite to all of them. Though nearly all the boys asked her out on dates, she refused them all. Not because she did not want to date, but because her parents forbid her to go on unsupervised dates until she was sixteen, and they did not have the schedules that would allow them to accompany her and a suiter even when she reached the dating age.

Gerry Kline was one of the boys who hounded Mary to go out, and at times, he was somewhat aggressive about it. Mary shared that with Curtis during what had become at least twice weekly walks on the banks of Mud Creek.

"I don't particularly like him," she said during one walk. "He seems kind of mean. Sometimes, he scares me."

Curtis fully understood where she was coming from. But he did not share with her his difficulties with Gerry.

Those had slacked off in the first couple of months of that eighth-grade year. But Gerry, perhaps fueled by his frustrations at getting nowhere with Mary, renewed his campaign of harassment against Curtis, who he learned spent a lot of time with her when they were both in Hazard. He kept it subtle at first, but it grew in intensity as the year went on.

For his part, Curtis mostly took the abuse, using all the tricks Principal Bass had taught him to keep his emotions in check. However, with each example of Gerry's aggressive behavior toward Mary, Curtis' efforts to keep from lashing out grew harder and harder.

That summer, Curtis got a reprieve from Gerry's bullying as they were separated by eight miles. Curtis had also turned fourteen in March, which allowed him to find a summer job. With a recommendation from Walter, he got a job with a farmer, and that pleased him a great deal. One of those farmer's fields was the one adjacent to Curtis' home -- the one he had spent so much time watching.

He started working just in time to take part in the first cutting of hay. His task was to walk behind the mower and rake any stray stacks into the neat rows left behind. When the cutting was done at all the farmer's fields, they went back and baled the hay into seventy-five-pound bales bound with twine.

This time, Curtis and one other boy, two years older, jabbed handled hooks into each end of a bale and lifted it onto a flatbed truck where another hand stacked them. The boy helping Curtis with the bucking of the bales knew him from school. He was a casual friend of Gerry's but did not hang out with him much. He witnessed Gerry's bullying - not just of Curtis but of others - but took no part in it. However, he also took no action to stop it. He tended to agree with Gerry's assessment that Curtis was a weakling and a weirdo. But he couldn't care less.

This was also the summer of Curtis' growth spirt. He grew four inches, which made him a little gangly and, at times, clumsy as he got used to the new height. But he was a determined and hard worker. At first, he had trouble lifting and controlling the bales of hay. But with each one, his arms, shoulders and back became used to the weight and width of the bales, and it became easier. It also helped that his workmate told him to lift with his knees and not his back.

By the time they finished bucking the first field's bales, Curtis was outpacing the older boy.

When the second cutting was completed - just days before Curtis' first day of high school - he found the bucking of the hay added muscle to his arms, shoulders and legs. He was also heavier, but still slim, and his coordination was improving quickly. He let his fluffy dark brown hair grow so that it was covering his ears. His face had taken on more of a mature look; one would even call it boyishly handsome. His deep blue eyes could drill right through a person, holding their attention like a grappling hook.

He was not the only one who noticed.

"Curtis, you really are good-looking, and you've become buff," Mary told him out of the blue during a "river" walk.

She had also grown by two inches, but Curtis seemed to tower over her. She saw him blush as they walked, but he said nothing. Inside, however, he was delighted that she had noticed.

The new school year brought Curtis and Mary out of their own little world in Hazard back into their troubled world.

Although Gerry was a little taken aback by Curtis' change over the summer, while his own physical appearance had changed very little, he hesitated only a few days before beginning anew his campaign of bullying. Curtis' lack of response to the subtle taunts angered Gerry, and his jibes became a little more overt.

Mary, now by far the prettiest and shapeliest girl at Littlefield High School, received even more attention. She had been approached about joining the cheerleading squad, but she demurely declined. She was not interested in drawing any more attention to herself than her looks and physical appearance already were. She even started dressing more conservatively, trying to downplay her shape.

That did not stop the boys, as they knew what was under the more loose-fitting clothing. More offers for dates poured in. She considered spending as much time as she could during the school days with Curtis in the hopes it would give the impression they were dating. But she cared about him too much to use him as a prop.

But he noticed her irritation with the constant flirting from the boys. While he did not seek her out, he did keep his eyes on her from a distance. He was ready and willing to step in if any of the boys got out of hand.

Gerry, like most of the boys at school, was attracted to Mary and made several attempts to date her. Her rejection of his advances only fueled his desire for her. One day in the early winter, it came to a head.

Seeing her come out of a classroom near one of the building's exit doors, Gerry rushed up, took her by the arm and ushered her outside. It was a chilly day with about one inch of snow on the ground. He grabbed her other arm and pushed her up against the building's exterior brick wall.

Standing three inches taller, Gerry turned his rugged face down and got within an inch of hers. She saw the ragged nose where Curtis had broken it that day in the elementary school hallway, although she knew nothing of the incident. Mixed with the smell of fresh snow, Mary caught a whiff of his sweaty body scent. She wrinkled her nose.

"Why won't you go out with me?" Gerry barked.

"I don't want to go out with you," she answered, trying to sound unafraid but failing badly.

"Why?" he insisted, squeezing her arms tighter.

At that moment, they heard the exit door clank open, and Curtis stepped outside, keeping one hand on the door as an invitation for Mary to go back inside. But Gerry kept his grip on her arms.

"Get the fuck out of here, This has nothing to do with you," Gerry growled.

"Leave her alone," Curtis said in a loud whisper.

"Go fuck yourself, queer," Gerry said, squeezing Mary's arms tighter. Tears began to roll down her cheeks.

Curtis took two steps toward them, cutting the ten-foot distance in half. Gerry released Mary and brought his fists up in an offensive fighting position. Mary staggered to the door, opened it, but did not go inside.

"Come on, Curtis, let's go inside," she sobbed.

Curtis stood his ground but did not say a word. Suddenly, Gerry let out a yell and sprinted forward. Curtis instinctively side-stepped the side-armed right hook Gerry threw at him. Gerry's momentum made him plunge into the open door, smacking his hand into the end mechanism on the bar lock. He immediately cradled his right hand with his left and let loose with a stream of obscenities in full voice. That drew a crowd of students and a couple of teachers running for the doorway to see what the commotion was.

"That son-of-a-bitch broke my hand," Gerry yelled.

A teacher led Gerry into the school to have the hand looked at by the school nurse. Gerry left a trail of curse words in his wake.

"What happened?" the teacher asked Curtis.

"I was protecting Mary," he answered. "Gerry was hurting her."

"What did you do?" the teacher asked.

"Nothing. He hit his hand on the door," Curtis explained.

The teacher looked at Mary for confirmation. She nodded her head, still lightly sobbing. Curtis and Mary were ushered inside and to the principal's office, where, each separately, gave their version of events. Their stories matched almost exactly. Gerry was still in the nurse's office and had yet to reveal his side.

Bonnie found herself sitting in another principal's office. This time, she had to leave work early after getting the call from the high school.

Bernard Whitkowski, unlike Timothy Bass at the elementary school, was a hard-line disciplinarian. He had been at the high school for nearly 20 years and had built a reputation of quick and swift justice within the walls of his school.

Bonnie had heard of the reputation from her colleagues at the county courthouse who had children attending the school. All of them had had their own experiences with the principal, and none of them were pleasant. It was why she had considered enrolling Curtis at Loup City High School instead of Litchfield. But when she talked to her son about it, his preference was to go to Litchfield because he wanted to remain near his small circle of friends, and Mary would enroll there.

Now, however, Bonnie was preparing herself for some news that was not going to be pleasant - for her or Curtis.

After reviewing some papers in front of him, Whitkowski finally spoke.

"Your son was involved in an incident earlier today in which a student was seriously injured," he began from the plush office chair behind his oak desk. "The other student was taken to the hospital in Loup City with what could be a broken wrist."

"What exactly happened?" Bonnie asked as calmly as she could.

"According to the injured student, your son confronted him without provocation and then pushed him into a door with great force," Whitkowski said.

"And who was this student?" Bonnie asked, although she had a pretty good idea. While Curtis had told her nothing about Gerry's bullying, she had overheard him talking to Mary about it when she visited their home.

"That's confidential," the principal responded.

"It was Gerry Kline, wasn't it," Bonnie said. It was not really a question. Bonnie had asked her son if there were any problems with other students, without mentioning Gerry, but Curtis said there had been only insignificant incidents since the matter at the elementary school.

"Again, that's confidential," Whitkowski said.

"And what did my son say happened?" Bonnie asked.

"All he said was he was protecting someone," the principal answered.

"Who?" Bonnie asked, but again, she was pretty sure who it was.

"That's confi..." Whitkowski began.

"Yes, confidential, I know," Bonnie said with sarcasm so thick she could walk on it.

"In any case, the other student claims the injured student was the aggressor and actually injured himself," Whitkowski said. "But it has come to my attention that your son has been involved in aggressive violence at another of our schools, and he is bigger than the injured student, so I'm more inclined to believe he could have been in this case as well."

"Well, you're wrong," Bonnie said, standing up. Whitkowski also stood.

"That, Ms. Herden, will be determined by law enforcement," the principal said brusquely. "I have been in contact with the injured student's parents, and they plan to press assault charges."

That was a turn of events she had not been prepared for. But standing there facing this principal, Bonnie decided it was time for another call to Sheriff Jesse Moore in Albany County. She only hoped he was still in office.

"In the meantime, Curtis is suspended for one week, beginning today," Whitkowski said, sitting back in his chair with an appearance as if the meeting was concluded.

"And what happens to this 'unnamed' injured student? You have a witness that claims he was the one who started things," Bonnie asked. Whitkowski looked up at her, clearly annoyed.

"He is being treated for his injury and likely will miss a day or two of school. After the sheriff's office finishes with their investigation, we'll see if any other action is required," he said, not even looking at Bonnie this time. "Now, if you will excuse me, I have a lot of work to do."

Bonnie stormed out, not bothering to tell Whitkowski what an asshole she thought he was.

Chapter 20

The Sherman County Sheriff's Office investigation into the assault charge brought against Curtis was completed before his week's suspension from school was over. Deputies interviewed all parties involved, including Whitkowski, within a couple of days of the charge being filed. They quickly conferred with each other and the sheriff to come to a determination.

Bonnie had called Sheriff Moore in Wyoming, asking that he speak to his Nebraska counterpart on Curtis' behalf.

"Ms. Herden, I don't know what I could add to their investigation, but I would be happy to share with them what you and your son went through here, if they are interested," He had told her. "But keep in mind that I may have to share what your former husband was into and what happened to him."

"I understand," Bonnie answered. "But you know what kind of boy Curtis is, and this move here has been so good for him."

"I'll do what I can," the Sheriff said.

Bonnie hoped the full story of the Albany killing, especially Curtis' involvement, did not have to be told. But if Sheriff Moore's words helped her son in any way, she would deal with any other consequences that came her way.

Sherman County Sheriff Bradley Stein did ask some questions that forced Moore to reveal that Delgado had been involved in drug and human smuggling, and that Bonnie had killed him in self-defense when the man was in a drunken rage and she was afraid he might harm or kill her son. But Moore left out the fact that Curtis was in the room at the time and that he claimed to have delivered all the stabs, including the final wound.

"So, you don't think the boy picked up his stepfather's violent tendencies?" Stein asked.

"Not at all," Moore said. "He did have a scrap at his school when a boy was bullying him, and Ms. Herden told me a similar thing happened there."

"That pattern could tend to work against him," Stein said. "But our information from the elementary school principal here indicates the other boy involved was the instigator. And the story from our witness to this latest incident matches Curtis', although it took a bit to get him to give us the details."

"I'm not surprised," Moore said. "What he went through here, losing his father so young and then having his mother in jail for killing the stepfather, turned him into a very introverted boy. That's why Ms. Herden's lawyer and I suggested they move away. Get away from the bad memories."

"Well, our take on this incident is the accusation of assault is baseless," Stein said. "This other kid hurt himself."

Moore was happy to hear that news, and called Bonnie to tell her as soon as his call with Sheriff Stein was done.

While the sheriff's investigation was concluded and the assault charge against Curtis was dropped, that was not the end of his troubles, both legal and otherwise.

During that first year of high school, Curtis focused solely on his schoolwork. He did not participate in any extra-curricular activities, including sports, although he did have an interest. When his after-school work schedule allowed, he attended Spartan games. But a lot of his motivation was to see Mary, who attended all the games.

Believing it would help with his social development, Bonnie constantly encouraged her son to get involved in other activities. But he continued on his chosen course.

However, as his second year in high school approached, Curtis became more interested in participating in sports. He first turned his attention to football. But Gerry had played on the Spartan team the year before and was certain to return, with his broken wrist fully healed. Curtis decided against going out for the sport. Not in fear of being hurt by Gerry, who he was certain would use the rough and violent sport as an excuse to legitimately inflict bodily harm upon him. No, Curtis was more concerned about losing his emotional control and injuring Gerry.

He considered wrestling and basketball. But the intimacy of wrestling did not appeal to him, and Gerry also played basketball, so he did not go out for that sport to avoid being near his tormentor.

Curtis did join a science club and a reading group, both because Mary was involved in each, and he had a specific interest in both subjects. And in the spring Mary talked him into joining the Spartans track and field team. She made a good argument that because it was more of an individual sport, he would really only be competing with himself for self-improvement. Besides, Gerry was a baseball player, so Curtis did not have to be near him to participate.

In track, he threw the shot put and ran the 800 meters. He did well enough in both to place in the top three in several meets and came within one place of qualifying for the state championship meet in the 800. Mary, helping the team as an equipment manager, was at each meet, including ones at other school locations, to cheer him on. That helped spur him to the self-improvement of which she had spoken. It also helped boost his self-confidence.

However, he remained uncomfortable getting into deep conversations with the other students, which kept his circle of friends small. Mary was the exception to his shyness for conversation.

During their "river" walks -- he still called Mud Creek a river - he opened up to her about his past. He shared with her the details he had been told of his father's death, the killing of his stepfather, his mother's time in jail and his stepfather's illegal activities.

"I tried to take the blame for his murder so Mom didn't go to prison, but they wouldn't believe me," he had told her. It was the first time he had revealed that to anyone.

That unsuccessful act of compassion impressed Mary, and made her feel closer to him. She did not verbalize that sentiment, but one way she showed it was to be more open with him.

"I get so tired of boys always staring at me and flirting with me," she said. "I know all they want is sex."

While he cared for Mary deeply, Curtis had no conscious thoughts of having sex with her. Not that it was revolting to him. He was certain somewhere deep in his subconscious, the desire was there; it just had not yet surfaced. That was partially because he would not allow such thoughts to enter his conscious thought process. He did not want anything to adversely affect their friendship.

"Don't you want to have sex?" he asked timidly. As soon as it was out of his mouth, he wished he could take it back. It sounded to him as if he were making a pass at her.

But Mary took the question at face value.

"I do, someday, with the right guy," she said. "But not until I am married."

She also shared with Curtis her growing frustration with living in such an isolated area. She craved the opportunities available in a more populated environment.

"I want to see and do things in my life," she said. "I can't do that here."

Curtis had never thought about being anywhere else. His personality was such that he enjoyed the solitude Hazard offered.

"What would you like to see and do?" he asked.

Mary talked of the many things that were available in larger areas. Her community in Ohio had been similar to Litchfield and Loup City, so there were movie theaters, shopping centers and other activities. But she talked of bigger things, like Broadway plays, fine dining, travel and the like. She also wanted to get a college education.

"I want to see more of this country. I want to see more of the world," she said.

As she talked more, Curtis slowly began to see the appeal of spreading his own wings.

After a short period of quiet, while he recuperated from his broken wrist the year before, Gerry continued his harassment of Curtis. He used Curtis' avoidance of participating in sports as another weapon, calling him a coward and a pussy. It got to Curtis at first, but Mary's calming influence during their "river" walks helped him keep his anger in check.

The campaign continued into their second year at the school and beyond. As time went on, Gerry's jibes at Curtis became less subtle. From time to time, Whitkowski would catch him hurling insults at Curtis, or catch wind of it through the school's grapevine, and call Gerry into his office to admonish him for it. But since he rarely, if ever, received any real consequences for his actions, the harassment continued.

During their third year at the school, Curtis continued with his science club, reading group and track activities. In track, he saw more improvement, placing high enough in the district meet to advance to the state meet. He finished fifth in the shot and sixth in the 800. Mary was there for it all.

After she turned 16, past her parents' benchmark for unsupervised dating, Mary had gone on a few outings with different boys. She did not date any boy more than once, and Gerry, though he kept trying, was never one of them. While she and Curtis never went on an official date, they continued to spend a great deal of time together.

Each time she did go on a date, Curtis felt a small bit of jealousy. He was a little confused by the feelings because he was spending more time with her than any of the guys she dated. So, why would he be jealous? He did not believe he was in love with her, nor she him. Or were they? He had never experienced romantic love, so he had no frame of reference.

There were times during their walks when he wanted to broach the subject. But he couldn't bring himself to do so. Would such a conversation drive her away from him? He was not willing to take that chance.

To complicate matters for Curtis, Bonnie, during his junior year in high school, had met a man in Loup City that she began seeing on a regular basis.

She had not intended to ever date anyone again. When she looked back on her history, she believed there was only one man who held her heart, and that was her first husband, Vince. But fate had taken him away from her. After that tragedy, she vowed not to get involved with another man.

But most people prefer the companionship that comes with a romantic relationship. Bonnie was one of those people. However, she let her loneliness at the time cloud her judgement, and she fell for Degado's charms, only to find out it was a facade. Once again, when Delgado was out of the picture, she vowed to avoid romance and concentrate on raising her son.

As Curtis neared the age where he would likely leave home to be on his own, that need for companionship again took hold.

She had talked to her son before starting the relationship. She wanted him to understand. She also wanted his approval.

"Mom, I want you to be happy," he said, after his mother's lengthy explanation. "If he makes you happy, I'm all for it."

She breathed a sigh of relief. But he was not finished. Bonnie was still an attractive woman, and he was worried about her.

"But I remember what happened the last time. Please make absolutely sure he is not just being nice so he can have sex with you," Curtis said. "And if he ever hurts you, I will go looking for him."

Bonnie was surprised at her son's frankness. And she felt proud of his protectiveness.

"I am being careful, Curtis," she said as she hugged him tightly. "I have a few more resources this time, and I'm not in the same frame of mind as before."

In the late fall of Curtis' senior year in high school, Bonnie decided to get rid of Delgado's pickup and get a new vehicle.

The truck had served her well over the years, but she felt it was time to rid herself of that last connection to the man she had come to despise. She had put enough money aside for a good down payment on a new vehicle.

The Ford pickup only had a little more than one hundred thousand miles, and she had been very diligent about regular maintenance, so it also provided a decent trade-in value. During the Loup City dealer's inspection of the vehicle, they found a small metal box bolted to the underside of the truck bed near the drive shaft. Apparently, during the cursory search by the Albany County deputies years before and numerous oil changes since, no one had paid it much mind. They all had figured it was part of the vehicle. And as it turned out the box was made of lead, so the Albany County Sheriff's Office X-ray machine could not detect anything inside it.

But the better trained and more experienced mechanics at the dealership knew the box served no purpose to the truck.

With Bonnie's permission, they unbolted the brackets that held the one-half-foot square box in place. The top was a hinged lid secured by a small lock. Bonnie had no key for it, so, again, with her permission, they pried it open. Bonnie and two mechanics stared in shock at the contents - neatly stacked piles of paper money held tightly by thick rubber bands.

"Holy shit!" one mechanic exclaimed, and they both looked at Bonnie. But she said nothing.

"How long has this been there? How much is in here?" the other mechanic asked.

"I don't know. My ex-husband must have put it there, probably ten or eleven years ago," Bonnie said.

"Then we should let him know we found it," a mechanic said. "How do we get ahold of him?"

"You can't, he's dead," Bonnie said absently, still a little shocked at the discovery. "I killed him," she heard herself say and immediately regretted it.

"Call the police," the older mechanic told the younger one.

Bonnie pulled out her cell phone and immediately dialed Sheriff Moore's number. She explained what they had found. He instructed her to stay where she was, and he would contact the Loup City police. He explained to them that the money, which had been missed by his deputies in a search of the truck ten years ago, was part of an ongoing drug and human smuggling investigation. He arranged to have the boxful of money, which turned out to be twenty-seven thousand dollars in various denominations, but mostly one-hundred dollar bills, shipped back to his office.

"Should we send the truck as well?" the manager asked.

"No, we have no need of the truck, since any evidence it might have had is tainted by now," Moore said, not wanting to leave Bonnie without a possible trade-in for the new vehicle she planned to purchase.

He explained all this to Bonnie later.

As it turned out, the dealership officials now wanted nothing to do with the Ford pickup. They said its involvement in possible illegal activities made it valueless, but they'd still be happy to sell her a car. The discovery of the money still shook Bonnie, but not enough to lose her feistiness.

"Screw you," she said, flashing her middle finger for the first time in her life. "I'll take my business elsewhere."

And she did, using the Ford as a trade-in for a brand-new Dodge Ram pickup truck.

As is typical in small rural towns, the information about the legal investigation Bonnie was connected to, and her faux pas of saying she killed Delgado, did not stay in the dealership. It filtered out into the wider community of Loup City.

While it did not affect her job at the county courthouse, since she had been forthright with them from the beginning, it did reach the gossipy ears of others. Through parents who had children attending Litchfield schools, the story spread there as well. And as is the case with gossip, each telling of the story twisted and exaggerated the so-called facts.

By the first of the year, it was common "knowledge" that Bonnie Herden was some kind of criminal. And by association, so was Curtis. The stories being told about them fueled Gerry's campaign of harassment, and drew others into his circle of influence.

The Jungs got wind of it and, while they were reluctant to believe all that they heard, having come to know Bonnie and Curtis as they had, they tended to the side of caution. They discouraged Mary from spending so much time with Curtis. She protested at first, but when her parents were insistent, she gave the appearance of going along.

Because Curtis had told her the entire story during their earlier walks, Mary fully supported Curtis and his mother. She even tried to debunk the stories that were circulating. But it had gone too far to stop the rolling juggernaut. The best she could do was try and deflect it a little bit.

Her defense of Curtis and Bonnie cost her friends, and people began to turn on her. Despite her parents' urgings that she sees less of Curtis, the events of those first few months of the year only prompted her to want to be with him even more. She talked him into sneaking out of their respective homes and meeting at their favorite spot -- the banks of Mud Creek -- at night.

Their walks and talks helped keep both their sanities intact. But it was at the end of one of these walks that their world came crashing down.

Chapter 21

Walking among the bur oak trees, with a few tulip poplar and bald cypress sprinkled here and there, that lined both sides of Mud Creek, always had a calming effect on Curtis. Once she joined Curtis in his "river" walking ritual, Mary understood its calming influence.

This night was no different.

They had been sneaking out for the walks for several weeks. Their parents had caught each of them a couple of times, and they promised not to do it again, a promise that was broken after a week's time since they had last been discovered. They made it a point to meet at the creek each Friday and Saturday night and, at most, two days during the week.

Their conversational topics varied, ranging from getting to know more about each other to their plans for the future to their current situation. The latter was the subject they tried to ignore because they did not want that to interfere with their special times together. But as the gossip continued, and increased in outrageousness, it was a hard subject to avoid.

This night, they agreed as soon as they met under the canopy of trees that the gossip and abuse directed at them would be a taboo subject. This night was for discussing their future plans.

It wasn't a new subject. They had talked about it before. Mary knew Curtis fancied himself as a farmer and he wanted to own his own land. Mary had made no secret of her desire to see and do more than Hazard -- or the rest of rural Nebraska -- had to offer. Their current difficulties had steeled her resolve. Curtis' aims remained the same, but he was now considering other locales.

"I might want to go back to Wyoming," he said softly as they slowly strolled north toward the creek's curve west, where it went under a bridge that took Nebraska Highway 10 over it.

"Why would you want to go back there?" Mary asked without judgment. "That's where all your troubles started."

Curtis thought about it a moment before responding.

"Yeah, but I wouldn't go back to Albany," he said.

"Where would you go?" she asked.

Another pause by Curtis followed.

"I've heard about this area on the other side of the state in the mountains with a lot of farms and ranches around a town called Dubois," he explained. "I did some research on the internet, and it seems nice."

"How big is this town -- Du Bois?" Mary asked.

"It's pronounced Dubois, like 'two boys,'" Curtis said with a smile. "About eight-hundred people live there, according to what I read."

"Are there any bigger cities close?" Mary asked.

They followed the curve of the creek.

"The biggest city in Wyoming is Casper and it is about 200 miles away," Curtis answered.

Mary mulled that for a few moments as they neared the bridge.

"So you want to cross over?" Curtis asked. Mary nodded her head but said nothing.

They walked through a space that had no trees. As they traversed that and crossed the bridge, they were silent as they looked up into the cloudless sky. They left the bridge and walked east along the creek bank to a point just opposite the space on the other bank with no trees. There was a small break in the trees on this side of the creek as well.

With hardly any ambient light coming from Hazard or anywhere for miles, the stars jumped out of the black of space around them. Mary invited Curtis to sit beside her and they stared up into the sky for about 15 minutes, just marveling at the vastness of the universe and the multitude of uncountable specks of light, some brighter than others.

As the hour approached eleven o'clock, there was very little activity. But they were serenaded by a chorus of crickets, and every few seconds they heard the soulful croak of a bullfrog somewhere near the bridge. Nature's musical concert stopped only briefly as a solitary car rolled down the highway and over the bridge. After it passed, the chirping and croaking continued.

"It doesn't sound like there is a lot to see and do there," Mary finally said.

At first, Curtis thought she was talking about outer space. He was about to argue that there could be thousands of inhabited worlds to explore when it dawned on him that she might be talking about their previous conversation.

"Wyoming? It's probably a lot like here," Curtis said.

"I'm not sure I'd like to go there," she whispered.

She uttered the remark apologetically, and Curtis recognized the sentiment. It caught him off guard. Knowing Mary as he had come to, he was certain she would not want to go to another area like Hazard. She had said on numerous occasions during their walks that she had higher aspirations. So why would she feel it necessary to tell him she would not want to go to Wyoming?

"I know you want to do and see more, so I don't think you would either," Curtis said.

Mary took his hand in hers and gave it a gentle squeeze. He felt his face flush a little, and he felt that familiar tightening in his jeans.

"God, Curtis, I wouldn't want to be away from you," she said, barely audible. "But there is more to this world I want to experience."

It was the first time Curtis had ever heard Mary express any reservations about being anywhere without him. He was not sure how to respond. Again, he did not want to risk saying anything that sounded like he was hitting on her for fear of turning her away from him. But it took all his will power to stifle the urge to express how he really felt about her.

"Where would you want to go?" he asked. He knew generally, because she had talked of seeing more of the country and the world. But it was the safest question he could think of at the moment.

"Well, I'd want to go to college, to start with," she said, continuing to hold his hand.

Curtis kept his head pointed to the sky. He wanted to look down and see her hand in his, but at the same time, he was afraid to look.

"Wouldn't you like to go to college?" Mary asked.

"Well, I think I know a lot about farming already, and I don't think I could learn more at a college," he said.

"That's not really true," she said. "Some colleges have great agricultural programs. I know that's true of the university in Nebraska."

That was something he had never considered. While in the moment, it sounded like it could be helpful for him, he knew even with the money he had saved and any his mother could contribute, he could not afford a college education that could cost as much as twenty-thousand dollars per year.

Bonnie had told him about the trust fund that would be his some day. But she had not shared the amount of funds in it. Besides, he had been planning to use money from the trust some day to buy his own farm.

"With your grades and your experience working on the farm here, I'm sure there are scholarships available," Mary said, guessing that he did not have the financial means for college from what she had learned about Curtis and Bonnie.

"Maybe we could go to the same college," Mary said hopefully.

"I haven't applied anywhere, and it's probably too late," he said.

"If you want to, I can help you find out," she offered.

"Okay," he said.

His response was so quick and casual that it took a moment for it to sink into Mary's consciousness. When it did, she squeezed his hand a little tighter, leaned over, and gave him a tender kiss on the cheek.

That gesture made his heart beat a bit faster, and he felt the heat in his face again indicating a blush. He was hopeful that it was dark enough that Mary did not notice. He slowly turned his head to face her. She was smiling, and there was almost a glow to her face.

"Mary, I..." Curtis stammered. But he quickly lost his nerve and looked away.

"What is it, Curtis?" she asked.

He said nothing for a few minutes. He could feel her anticipation of what he would say. But he couldn't bring himself to say what he really wanted to say.

"We should be getting home," he finally muttered.

Curtis felt Mary's hand release his, and his heart sank.

"You go ahead. I want to sit here for a while," she said gloomily.

"Are you sure?" he asked. "I don't feel right leaving you here alone."

"It's alright," she said. The sorrow in her voice melted his heart, but he still kept his true feelings inside. "I won't be long," she added.

Reluctantly, he stood and looked down at her. She was sitting cross-legged on the grass, her head turned toward her lap. He wanted to stay, but it seemed his refusal to finish telling her what he started offended her. He was not sure how to make it right. So he slowly walked south along the creek bank to a spot that was shallow enough that several rocks peaked above the surface of the slowly rolling water. He hopped on the rocks until he was on the other side.

He looked back and could see through a break in the tree umbrella back to where they had been sitting together. Mary was still sitting on the grass, her head down. She had her back to him so he did not see the tears streaming down her face.

Curtis crossed the field, then Nebraska Highway 2. He stopped and looked north, hoping to see Mary walking toward her home. But he saw no one - no walkers, no vehicle traffic, very few lights in buildings. Cursing himself for not having the courage to tell Mary just how much he loved her, he walked the rest of the way home and silently snuck back into the house.

Curtis was eager to get to school the following day. In the hours since he and Mary had sat on the creek bank, he had built up his courage. He wanted to say to her what he could not when they sat side by side, her hand in his.

Since Mary rode the bus to school, Curtis had joined her, rather than have his mother drop him off. But that morning, she had not been on the bus from Hazard and was not to be found once it deposited students at the high school. Not in the two classes they had together, not in the hallways between classes, not in the cafeteria during lunch.

Like Curtis, Mary rarely missed school. As with him, she was a good student, just a few slots behind him in the class standings. She was focused on her education. In the time he had known her, she had missed only a few days of school.

He had been with her until nearly midnight, and she showed no signs of being ill, so he was certain that was not why she was not attending school that day. It had been a bit chilly during the time they spent by the creek. But he did not believe it had been cold enough to make her sick, and she had worn a jacket and long pants.

Perhaps her parents had gone somewhere - maybe some kind of family emergency -- and taken her with them. As the day went on, other scenarios rattled through his head. Some that made him shudder and made him fret for her safety.

When the final bell rang, dismissing the students from the campus, Curtis went immediately to the bus to Hazard and got on board. The trip over the eight miles seemed to take forever. After stepping off the bus, he went to the porch and waited there, not even taking his backpack inside.

It was nearly six o'clock when Bonnie got home from work. She saw Curtis sitting on the porch swing with a worried look on his face.

"What's wrong?" she asked.

"Mary wasn't at school today. I'm worried," he answered.

"Maybe she was sick," his mother said, sitting down beside him. "Did you call her house?"

"I was afraid to," he said. "Her parents have been discouraging her from spending time with me. I thought they might be mad if I called."

"Well, I'm sure everything is alright," Bonnie said.

"But when I saw her last night, she was just fine," he said without thinking.

"When did you see her last night?" Bonnie asked, surprised. "You were home from the time you came from school until you went to bed."

Curtis realized that his mother thought that he had obeyed since he had been caught sneaking out a couple of times and been reprimanded for it. Now, he had to explain that their clandestine meetings had continued. That did not set well with Bonnie.

"I told you to stop sneaking out," she started, but went no further when she saw the Jungs' car pull into their driveway. Joachim and Ava bounded out and hurriedly went to the porch.

"Have you seen our daughter?" Joachim asked, looking alternately at Bonnie and Curtis.

"No, she has not been here, and Curtis said she was not at school today," Bonnie said. "We thought she was sick, or you all had gone somewhere."

Joachim and Ava both went pale. They had left the house and headed for their respective jobs before Mary's usual time to begin getting ready. That was the normal routine on weekdays.

"Curtis saw her last night and said she seemed fine then," Bonnie said.

Curtis' embarrassment was evident as he would now have to admit to the Jungs that he had been meeting their daughter regularly at night. He recounted what they had been doing and told them how the last evening had gone.

"Why did you leave her alone out there?" Ava asked through tears now flowing from her eyes.

"She told me to," Curtis said sheepishly.

"That was very irresponsible of you," Joachim said. "If anything has happened to her, you will be held accountable."

"Okay, let's settle down now," Bonnie said, standing up. "The first thing we need to do is call the police and report her missing."

She pulled out her cell phone and dialed the county sheriff's number. She handed the phone to Joachim and motioned Curtis to get out of the porch swing. Bonnie gently took Ava's arm and guided her to the seat, then motioned for Joachim to sit next to his wife, which he did while he made the call to the sheriff's office.

Chapter 22

Curtis was eager to go looking for Mary even as her father was on the phone with the sheriff's office. But Bonnie discouraged him, at least until Joachim was through with the call.

"Where would you look?" his mother asked.

"I would start where we were last night," Curtis said. "Then I would work my way toward her house. If something happened, it would be somewhere along there."

Bonnie could see the logic in his thinking. She was about ready to send him on the search when Joachim waved at them, the phone still pressed to his ear. He listened for another moment, then held the phone out for Curtis.

"You were with the missing girl last night?" he heard a deputy ask.

"Yes, sir," he answered. "We were down by the river talking."

"The river? There in Hazard?" the deputy asked. "There is no river there. Do you mean Mud Creek?" Curtis answered in the affirmative.

"Where are you now?" the deputy asked.

"I'm at home in Hazard," Curtis said, giving him the address.

"Stay where you are. We'll have someone there in about twenty minutes, and we want you to show the deputy where you and the girl were from the time you met up until you left her," the deputy instructed.

At those last few words, Curtis felt a wave of guilt come over him. He never should have left her all alone so late at night. He apologized to the Jungs. Ava continued to cry, and Joachim only glared at him. Curtis felt tears forming in his eyes. Not wanting the adults to see it, he walked off the porch and sat on one of the wooden lawn chairs, the same one he had plopped into to chat with Mary the day after he had first seen her walk by his house those years ago.

He felt the tears begin trickling out of his eyes, but he choked down the sound of his sobs.

When the deputy arrived, he and Curtis began their trek. Bonnie and the Jungs wanted to accompany them, but the deputy refused.

"I want you people to stay here in case the girl shows up," he said. "Besides, the fewer the people out there, the better."

What he left unsaid was that the fewer people traipsing around the creek reduced the risk of spoiling evidence in case it turned into a crime scene.

Deputy Blaine McNutt and Curtis crossed Nebraska Highway 2, then the railroad tracks. The passed north of the sewage pond and across the field, skirting a stand of trees before doing so. Curtis led McNutt into the trees lining the creek. They both slowly walked along the creek bank, around the curve and across the bridge on Nebraska Highway 10.

When they came to the small break in the trees where Curtis and Mary sat the night before, McNutt put his hand on Curtis' chest to hold him back.

"Stay right here," he told Curtis, then slowly moved a few steps forward.

Curtis watched as the deputy used his cell phone to take photos of the ground around where the two teens had been sitting. The sun was nearing the western horizon, but was still providing enough light to see the area clearly, though with a slight orange tint. He could see the ground was disturbed in a way that it had not been the night before. McNutt then walked a few yards downstream and took photos of something in the water.

Taking a wide arc around the area he had photographed, the deputy returned to Curtis and motioned for him to follow. They followed the same arcing path back to where the item was in the water.

"Do you recognize that?" the deputy asked, pointing.

Curtis felt his heart pounding against his chest, and his knees went a little wobbly.

"Th...that's Mary's...uh hum... jacket," he stuttered, the words sticking in his throat.

McNutt keyed the mic clipped to his shoulder.

"Send someone out to Mud Creek just east of the Highway 10 bridge with some evidence bags and the works. I think we've got a crime scene," he said.

Deputies interviewed Curtis, Bonnie and the Jungs late into the might. They spent most of their time with Curtis, grilling him over and over, asking the same things in different ways, trying to trip him up. But his story remained the same throughout.

The deputies finally gave up around midnight.

The following day, a Friday, Curtis was up early, getting ready for school as usual. Bonnie had not yet left for work and offered to drop him off at the high school. She was concerned about her son.

"No, thank you, Mom. I'll ride the bus," he said. It was a change he made when he entered high school. In addition to wanting to ride the bus with Mary, he felt self-conscious having his mother drop him off now that he was older.

"Are you okay?" she asked.

He looked tired, which was understandable considering how late he had gone to bed. But then again, now that she knew he had been sneaking out late at night, she believed lack of sleep was not the problem.

"I didn't do anything to Mary, Mom," he said. "I really liked her."

"I know, Baby. I'm sure you didn't do anything to her," his mother responded.

"But they probably think I did. I know how it looks," he said.

Bonnie swallowed the lump down her throat and fought hard to keep from crying.

"They will find her safe. I just know it," she stammered.

Curtis went to his mother and gave her a hug.

"I hope so," he said. "I'm worried about her."

Curtis' ride to school on the bus was uneventful. However, most high school-age riders gave him scornful and accusing looks when he climbed aboard and through most of the trip. Not much changed when he debarked at the school. He did notice several county sheriff vehicles in the parking lot.

Throughout the day, Curtis noticed, whenever he was out of class and near the administrative offices, students going into the principal's office in twos and threes. He also saw some of them coming out. The boys who exited looked angry, and if they noticed Curtis, they shot daggers at him. The girls came out crying.

He did catch sight of Gerry heading into the office with two girls. Gerry saw Curtis out of the corner of his eye, and a sadistic smile creeped across his lips.

Curtis judged all his observations, especially Gerry's obvious satisfaction, as ominous signs. He also noticed that even his small circle of close friends were giving him a wide berth.

Sitting in his last class of the day, with just fifteen minutes before the final bell, he heard a knock at the door, interrupting the teacher in mid-sentence. Curtis felt a shiver go through him. After a very brief discussion at the door, the teacher motioned for Curtis to come forward.

"Bring your backpack," the teacher instructed.

As he walked up to the classroom door, Curtis saw not one, not two, but three sheriff's deputies standing in the hallway, one standing in front of the other two with a pair of handcuffs in his hand. The other two deputies had their hands on the butts of their holstered pistols.

The lead deputy reached out and roughly took Curtis' backpack and handed it to one of the other deputies, who took it in his off-hand, keeping the other on his gun. Curtis started to protest but thought better of it.

"Curtis Herden, you'll be coming with us," the lead deputy said. "We have more questions for you about the disappearance of Ruth Jung."

The teacher stepped forward and pulled the door nearly shut behind him. He noticed that some students had gotten out of their seats and moved toward the front of the classroom to get a better look at what was going on.

"Are those really necessary?" the teacher asked, pointing at the handcuffs.

"Yes, we believe they are," the deputy said while motioning for Curtis to turn around, which he did, putting his hands behind his back. He heard the cuffs click shut, but they weren't as tight on his wrists as he had expected.

"I need to call my mom," Curtis said as they marched him down he hallway toward the main entrance. As they passed classrooms, students rushed to the doors and spilled out into the hallway, with their teachers chastising them to return to their seats.

"She has been notified," the lead deputy said, not even hesitating his march for an instant.

"Is my son under arrest?" Bonnie fumed when she saw the deputies come into the sheriff's substation in Loup City.

"He is not formally under arrest at the moment, but that could change," the deputy said.

The other two deputies stood a few feet away on each side of Curtis. Bonnie could read the worry in his expression.

"Then why is he handcuffed?" Bonnie demanded.

The lead deputy cursed himself for not removing them before coming in the door. But he was not expecting to be confronted by an angry parent so quickly.

"Ms. Herden, based on information we gathered at the school, we believed it was prudent," he said as he removed the cuffs. "We have some further questions for him." Bonnie opened her mouth to protest that they had spent most of the night questioning him, but the deputy held up his index finger to stop her. "After we are done, we'll make a determination about an arrest."

"He gave you all the information he had last night. Now, he won't say another thing until a lawyer is with him," Bonnie said, glancing at Curtis, who gave a reassuring nod.

"That is his right," the deputy said. "But we're going to ask our questions anyway." He quickly motioned for the other deputies to take Curtis to a small interview room, and they all hustled off, leaving Bonnie standing in the lobby.

Once in the interview room, the lead deputy and a detective sat in rolling office chairs at the end of a small rectangular table pushed into a corner while Curtis was in a hard, unpadded metal folding chair on the long end of the table. The detective read the Miranda rights to Curtis slowly and deliberately.

"Do you understand these rights as I have explained them?" he asked.

"Yes, sir," Curtis said politely.

"Do you want to invoke your right to remain silent?" he asked.

Curtis did not answer, not wanting to say the wrong thing. The two officers looked at each other and shrugged. They began peppering Curtis with questions. Most were the same as he had answered the night before, but there were some new ones. Throughout their queries, Curtis sat ramrod straight in the uncomfortable chair, as stoic as a statue.

After about thirty minutes, there was a light tapping on the door. The deputy opened the door, listened for a moment, then motioned for the detective to follow him out of the room. Then, in walked a tall, thin man in a rumpled business suit, with Bonnie trailing behind. They took the seats the officers had been sitting in. But the man, who was in his fifties with salt and pepper hair and a neatly trimmed beard and mustache of the same coloring, quickly rose and motioned for Curtis to take his seat, and he sat in the metal chair.

"I am Matthew Dunbar. But please call me Matt," he said, presenting his hand to Curtis, who shook it firmly. "I'll be your lawyer."

After a brief discussion, Dunbar went to the door and called for the detective, who entered with the same deputy. They brought in another rolling office chair and ushered Bonnie out of the room, which she was none too pleased about. The detective ordered Curtis back into the metal chair.

"I'm good where I am," Dunbar said. "Curtis, roll your chair over here and sit next to me."

The detective and deputy scowled at the attorney, but did not push the matter. They quickly sat down and began their questioning. Curtis, each time consulting Dunbar first, answered every question, spinning the same scenario he had given the night before. All the new questions regarded his trouble at the Centennial Elementary School and the confrontations with Gerry at Litchfield. Curtis answered each question truthfully, despite some of the "facts" as presented by the officers being exaggerated or blatantly false.

The questioning, with many of the inquiries repeated or asked in different ways, continued for nearly three hours. Finally, Dunbar had had enough.

"Gentlemen, I believe my client has answered all of your questions repeatedly," he said a little testily. "Now, unless you have some real evidence to justify an arrest, we'll be leaving."

Dunbar stood and indicated for Curtis to do the same, which he did.

"We do have the girl's jacket that was discarded at the creek," the detective said. "It was cold that night, so why would she leave it behind unless she was forced to?"

Dunbar looked the detective in the eye, fixing him with a steely gaze that the other man instinctively tried to avoid.

"And are my client's fingerprints or DNA on that jacket?" the lawyer asked.

"Well, no," the detective said. "But it was submerged in the creek water, and we're still testing it."

"Is there any physical evidence linking my client to any crime?" Dunbar asked, emphasizing the word "any" both times.

"Not at this time," the detective sheepishly answered. "But our interviews at the high school have indicated your client has a temper and a history of animosity and violence."

"My information indicates the 'violence' you speak of are two incidents in which my client was the target of a bully in one, and he was protecting another student in the other, and the so-called victim actually hurt himself," Dunbar said coldly.

"So all you have is circumstantial evidence and gossip," Dunbar said. "We'll be leaving."

The lawyer, calmly, and Curtis, cautiously relieved, walked out of the interview room and joined Bonnie in the lobby. They retrieved Curtis' backpack from the property clerk and left the substation.

Chapter 23

Curtis was up early the following morning. He was headed for the farm where he worked. He was planning to spend the day on the farm working as hard as he could. He was hoping the work would help take his mind off Mary's disappearance and the suspicion that was being leveled at him.

But when he got to the farmer's barn, his boss, Ben Childers, told him to go home.

"I don't have anything for you to do today," he said, looking Curtis directly in the eye.

"But don't you have three fields to irrigate?" Curtis asked.

"I have it all covered," Childers said matter-of-factly.

"Should I come back tomorrow?" Curtis asked, hoping the answer would be yes.

"No, it's covered," Childers said.

"Are you firing me?" Curtis asked, emotion starting to build up.

"No, Curtis, I'm not," Childers said, a little sympathy seeping out of his facial expression. "I just..."

"You think I've done something wrong," Curtis said with a mixture of anger and sadness.

"I know the Jung girl is missing and that you two were close friends. I just think your mind won't be totally on your work," Childers said. "And I think you could use a couple of days off to get your head straight."

"Fine," Curtis shot back. He turned and began walking home before frustration, resentment and anger building in him burst out.

Childers watched him go with a touch of sadness in his heart. In the time Curtis had worked for him, he had become fond of the young man. He was hard working -- harder than anyone else - and he was honest. He certainly could have used Curtis' help that day.

But Childers was also cautious enough to cover his ass. As much as he liked Curtis, he needed to protect himself and his farm operation from any consequences of having Curtis around if he was found to be responsible for any wrongdoing.

It didn't make him feel good about his decision, though.

By the time he neared home, Curtis had made up his mind that he was going to go search for Mary. He had no idea where to look, but he felt he had to do something. He could not stand just doing nothing while she was missing. Track practice had started two weeks previously, and the first competitive meet was scheduled for the following weekend. But that was the farthest thing from Curtis' mind.

He had wanted to begin searching for Mary the night before. But Bonnie talked him out of it.

"I don't want you out there by yourself," Bonnie had said.

"But, Mom, I need to find her. She could be hurt," he argued.

"That is a possibility," she responded firmly. "But the sheriff's office will be looking for her, and we shouldn't get in the way."

"They don't have enough people to look for her. They need help," Curtis persisted.

"That is also a possibility," Bonnie said. "And if they ask for help, you and I both can volunteer."

He started to protest again, but she silenced him with a gentle hand on his shoulder.

"That's the way it has to be," she said. "And no sneaking out."

As much as he wanted to do otherwise, he resisted the temptation to disobey his mother.

Curtis was not happy at being left out of a search for Mary, but since Mr. Childers was not going to allow him to work on the farm, his determination to be involved in a search returned.

However, when he saw a sheriff's car parked in the driveway, he entered the house and found his mother sitting in the living room with two deputies. Bonnie quickly got up and directed Curtis to a seat next to her on the couch against the front window. The deputies sat against the wall to their right, one in an easy chair and the other in an old-fashioned wooden rocking chair Bonnie had found at an antique store in Loup City.

"The sheriff's office is asking for volunteers to help in their search," Bonnie said. Curtis turned to the deputies with a look of anticipation and began to offer his services, but Bonnie spoke before he could, putting a hand on his shoulder. "They don't want you involved."

Curtis looked at his mother, puzzled, then back at the deputies with fire in his eyes.

"Why the hell not?" he hissed through clenched teeth. Bonnie, who had never heard him use any swear word before in his life, tightened her grip on his shoulder, and he heard her whisper, "Curtis, settle down." But he couldn't.

"Curtis, you are a person of interest in this girl's disappearance," One deputy said slowly and carefully. "We believe it will be counterproductive for you to be involved in a search."

"She was safe and sound by the river when I left. I didn't do anything to hurt her," Curtis was almost yelling.

"That could be true..." the deputy began.

"It is true. She was my best friend. I would never do anything to hurt her," Curtis said, raising his voice another octave. Bonnie squeezed his shoulder again.

"As I started to say, that may be true, but we won't know for sure until we find her," the deputy said. His partner sat silently observing.

"I didn't do anything to her," Curtis said, his voice dropping to its normal tone and volume.

"Your mother said you had gone to work this morning," the deputy said. "So why did you come home?"

"Mr. Childers doesn't want me to work this weekend. I think he's firing me," Curtis said, a little bitterness between the words.

"Why do you think that?" the deputy asked.

"Because this is the time when he gets busier with the hay crop," Curtis said absently.

"Maybe he just knows you need time off to deal with all this," the deputy said.

"Or maybe, like you guys and everyone else, he thinks I'm guilty of something," Curtis said, the anger returning to his voice. He stood up, marched out of the living room, and went to his bedroom. The slamming door rattled the windows.

"Ms. Herden, we're not judging Curtis guilty," the deputy said as both officers stood up in unison. "We're just trying to do our jobs and find this girl."

"Well, it sure doesn't seem like it to Curtis. Or to me," Bonnie said, still sitting on the couch and glaring at the deputies.

They quietly excused themselves and left the house.

While Curtis was housebound for the rest of the weekend, sheriff's deputies and about forty volunteers searched the area for any sign of Mary. Joachim and Ava Jung were among the volunteers, as was Gerry Kline.

The small army started with the site where Curtis claimed he last saw Mary and worked its way outward. All homes and businesses in Hazard were searched, including Bonnie's home and property. A group of ten volunteers was also dispatched to Ben Childers' farm - all four hundred acres, including the fields, houses, barn and all other outbuildings. Childers was not happy. The searchers disrupted his work and tamped down the hay in the fields.

The search was conducted all day Saturday and, after a night's break, all day Sunday.

Sheriff's deputies also canvassed the area interviewing residents, hoping they would find someone who saw something that night. But that and the searches brought absolutely no results by the end of the weekend.

Curtis returned to school on Monday. He faced a hostile environment. Word of his questioning by deputies had spread, and so did more talk of his mother's jail time in Wyoming.

This time Bonnie had insisted on taking him to school and had dropped him off on her way to work and planned to pick him up at the end of the day, even leaving work early so he didn't have to wait on the campus.

His schoolmates, now including his small group of friends, looked at him with great suspicion and contempt. Most were convinced he had something to do with Mary's disappearance. No one was more convinced than Gerry Kline.

"There goes the kidnapper, the murderer," he said loudly the first time he saw Curtis in the hallway of the school.

"What did you do to her, freak?" he hollered at the next encounter.

"You're going to pay for what you did, jerkoff," he snarled into Curtis' face another time.

Gerry did not get physical with Curtis during these encounters. But he could tell he was getting under Curtis' skin. For his part, Curtis controlled his reactions, including saying nothing in response. However, with each encounter it was becoming more difficult to keep from responding in some way.

At the end of the day, he gathered his things and headed for the parking lot. Gerry followed him, peppering him with more accusations and abuse. As Curtis was nearing Bonnie's car, she got out and pointed a finger at Gerry.

"You leave him alone," she shouted.

"Shut up, you murdering bitch. We know what you did to your husband," Gerry yelled. "Like mother like son."

A crowd of students and a sprinkling of school staff had gathered nearby. Some were egging Gerry on. Others just watched silently, but with anger in their eyes directed at Curtis and Bonnie.

When Gerry lashed out at his mother, Curtis' resolve vanished. He turned and advanced on Gerry menacingly.

"You leave my mother alone, you son-of-a-bitch," he screamed.

"What are you going to do about it, fag boy?" Gerry taunted.

Without saying a word, Curtis cocked his arm and sent his fist rocketing toward Gerry's face. The antagonist tried to block the blow but was not fast enough, and Curtis connected right under Gerry's left eye. The blow sent him sprawling to the ground.

Bonnie rushed over and grabbed her son by both arms and turned him toward the car. Wordlessly, she forced him to get in the passenger seat and then got in the other side. She did a mini burnout as she left the parking lot.

Later that night, a sheriff's deputy visited the Herden home and informed Bonnie and Curtis that no charges were going to be filed for the incident in the school parking lot.

"Our school resource officer witnessed the incident and indicated that the other boy was the instigator," he said, then turned his attention to Curtis. "That being said, your reaction will not be ignored."

Bonnie went to the door and opened it.

"Thank you for letting us know," she said, frustration clearly visible on her face. "Now, I'd like to talk to my son."

"One more thing, Curtis has been expelled from school," the deputy said as he walked toward the yawning doorway. "Not just Litchfield, but any school in the district."

"So my son has been judged guilty without any trial," Bonnie snapped back, bitterness dripping from her lips.

The deputy did not even turn around as he headed for his patrol car. He knew that as far as residents in Hazard and Litchfield were concerned, Bonnie had hit the nail squarely on the head.

After a weekend of being stuck at home and the day he had at school, Curtis had to get out for a while. He waited until he knew Bonnie was sound asleep, then snuck out his usual way and headed for Mud Creek. He was so intent on his short journey that he paid no mind to the unfamiliar car parked just down the street from his home.

When Curtis appeared on the street headed south, the driver of that car crouched down behind the steering wheel so as not to be seen. The driver did not need to look up to see where Curtis was going. That was already known. Fingers keyed numbers on a cell phone.

"He is headed there now. Stay out of sight until I get there," the driver said when the call was answered.

The driver waited until Curtis disappeared into the stand of trees by the sewage pond, then started the car and moved down the street to make a sharp right onto the street that paralleled Highway 2. At Seventy-seventh Road, the driver turned left and, just after crossing Highway 10, turned onto an access space between the highway and an adjacent field, parking at the north end of the bridge over Mud Creek.

Curtis heard the car make its short trek, but paid it no mind. There was always some isolated traffic late at night, most times farmers checking something on their fields or changing irrigation patterns.

He crossed the creek at the shallow point with the stone path across. This time, he did not stay within the tree line along the creek bank but walked across the open clearing to the point at the curve in the creek where he had last seen Mary. The bright yellow crime scene tape was still there. It had been windy during the weekend and the strand right in front of him had blown loose and was fluttering in the slight breeze that remained.

He stood looking at the spot where he and Mary had been sitting just nights before. He silently cursed himself for not telling her what he had longed to for months. Maybe if he had, she would be here with him now.

"I shouldn't have left her here alone," he whispered.

Suddenly, he heard rustling noises coming from his left. When he looked in that direction, he saw Gerry Kline emerge from the darkness. He snapped his fingers once, and Curtis was aware of movement behind him. He turned his head and saw what seemed to be ten shadowy figures, two or three with objects in their hands. He turned back to Gerry and noticed that in his right hand was what looked like an aluminum baseball bat.

"You're going to tell us what you did to Mary," Gerry said menacingly, taking a few steps toward him. Curtis sensed the others behind him closing in as well.

"I don't know where she is or what happened to her," Curtis said firmly, feeling the adrenaline pumping in his body.

Gerry took a swing with the bat, and although Curtis attempted to duck under it, the bat connected with a sloid blow to his left shoulder, knocking him off balance. He was able to right himself, but before he could react, he felt fists slamming into his lower back, both his sides and one to his right ear.

"Where is she?" he heard Gerry hiss in a half-whisper.

The aluminum bat smashed into his abdomen, sending a great gush of air out of him. He fought to catch his breath but could not get any oxygen to come into his lungs. His vision began to blur, and he felt his knees start to sag when a pipe crashed into the back of his calves in a forward arc. His feet were taken out from under him. What little air there was still in his lungs went whooshing out of him when he landed flat on his back. He could vaguely feel more punches and kicks to his head, sides and chest before he passed out.

Curtis was uncertain how much time had passed before he came to, gasping for air. As he pulled in great amounts of oxygen from the night air, his vision slowly returned and he was looking up at a sky full of stars ringed by a multitude of faces looking down at him.

"He's not going to tell us anything. Lets just leave him here," he heard a voice say.

"No," Gerry yelled.

Curtis saw the face that he had come to despise looking down at him.

"Where the hell is Mary? What the fuck have you done to her?' Gerry demanded.

"I don't know," was Curtis' weak response.

"The hell you don't," Gerry hollered and raised the bat over his right shoulder.

Curtis instinctively turned his head to the right and tried to raise his hands to protect his face. But they would not move, as they were pinned to the ground by boys on either side. Gerry's full force swing of the bat caught Curtis squarely on the left temple. Almost simultaneously, he was struck in the back of the head with a pipe.

Both blows came with such force that the temple impact caused a bone fragment to be forced into the brain and the head shot severely cracked the skull and jostled Curtis' brain so violently that it immediately started to swell. Gerry was so worked up that he sent a second blow that connected just above Curtis' left ear. This one did create a small skull fracture but also tore off a piece of scalp that immediately started to bleed profusely. Gerry hauled back for another swing, but two of the boys grabbed the bat and stopped the momentum.

"That's enough," one of them said.

Even in the darkness, they could see the blood gushing from Curtis' head wound. They could also see he was not moving.

"We need to call an ambulance," one of the boys said.

"No, we need to get the hell out of here," Gerry said as he turned toward the bridge. "That cock-sucker got what he deserved."

Curtis did not hear the scurrying of feet or the splashing of the water as some of the boys ran through the creek to get to their vehicles parked in Hazard. The only thing he was aware of was the image of him and Mary sitting beside Mud Creek holding hands. Her beautiful face was smiling at him. He heard his own voice, but he could not make out the words. Then he saw Mary's smile widen, and she threw her arms around him.

It was at that moment the image slowly faded like the end of a classic movie and then it was gone.

Chapter 24

Bonnie's eyes fluttered open, and she lifted her head from the pillow. Looking toward the night stand her still blurry vision seemed to show the digital alarm clock's numbers read 3:11. Fearing she had slept through the day and missed work, she was suddenly more awake. But the darkness in the room told her it was still morning.

She then heard five loud bangs that seemed to come from the front of the house. Bonnie raised herself onto her elbow and listened carefully. A few seconds later, the same five bangs sounded. She recognized it as someone knocking on the front door jam.

Bonnie pushed her body out of the bed and got to her feet. She headed for the bedroom door but suddenly realized that because of the heat, she had slept only in her panties. She went to the closet, pulled out a light blue satin robe, threw her arms into the sleeves, and wrapped the rest around her nearly nude body. She knotted the tie around her waist as she headed for the front door, as the pounding was renewed.

She flicked on the porch light and opened the main door. Through the screen door, she saw two sheriff's deputies stand outside. They had very serious looks on their faces.

"What do you want with Curtis now?" she spat.

The deputies both looked down at their boots.

"It's not that, Ms. Herden..." one deputy said, looking up but hesitating.

"Did you find Mary?" Bonnie asked, this time with some hope in her voice.

"No, ma'am, we haven't," the same deputy said. "May we come in?"

Bonnie was puzzled. Why were these deputies at her home at three o'clock in the morning? She also wondered why Curtis, who she had learned through the years was a light sleeper, had not ventured out of his bedroom to see what the noise was. For that matter, why had he not gotten up to answer the door?

Despite her confusion, she did not want to be rude to these deputies, since they claimed they weren't there to grill her son some more about his missing friend. She turned on the living room light and unlocked the screen door. One of the deputies opened the door and they both slowly walked inside.

"Ms. Herden, please sit down," a deputy said, putting his hand lightly on her arm and guiding her to the couch. Still trying to clear her sleep-dulled brain, she sat down, never taking her eyes off him as he sat next to her. The other deputy sat in one of the chairs.

"Ms. Herden, I am sorry to have to tell you this, but we found your son..." the deputy next to her began, but she was quick to respond before he could finish.

"Oh no, he's asleep in his room," she said, pointing toward his bedroom, but still locking eyes with the officer.

"No, Ms. Herden, we found him by the creek," he said, working hard to keep his composure. "He is dead."

Bonnie heard the words, but they made no sense to her. She had specifically told Curtis he was not allowed to sneak out at night. Despite the fact that he had been doing it for weeks to see Mary, and he was so determined to go searching for her now, she believed he would not have disobeyed her this time.

She slowly got up and began walking toward his bedroom. Both deputies got up and followed her. She lightly tapped on his door and called his name. When there was no answer, she knocked harder and said his name louder. When there was still no response, she opened the door and turned on the light.

In front of her was a room with no occupant. His bed was neatly made, as if he had not slept in it. Finally, what the deputy had said to her in the living room became very clear in her mind. She felt dizzy and began gasping for breath. She felt a firm hand take hold of her arm as her knees went weak. The last thing she remembered was seeing the floor come rushing toward her.

Bonnie was lying on the floor when she came to. One deputy was on one knee next to her, and the other was standing in the short hallway between the two bedrooms. She was on her back and could feel a large, rough hand on hers. She blinked a couple of times and looked at the kneeling deputy.

"Are you okay?" he asked. "You fainted."

She nodded her head to indicate she was conscious.

"Did you tell me my son is dead?" she asked.

"Yes, ma'am, he was out by the creek and had his identification in his wallet," he answered carefully. "But we need you to positively identify him, if you are up to it."

Bonnie began to sit up, and the deputy put his hand on her back to help her. The other deputy came forward and extended his hand to help her up. As he gently pulled her forward, she curled her legs underneath her and stood. She was still a little dizzy.

"What do I have to do?" she asked, with a calmness that puzzled the deputies. She had seen enough cop shows on television with scenes of family members viewing bodies. But this was reality -- and her son. As much as she wanted to cry, scream, lash out -- anything to release the initial grief - she knew this was not the time. There was also anger building up in her that helped push that grief to the side.

Being careful not to use the term "the body" to avoid dehumanizing the boy to his mother, the deputy explained that Curtis had been taken to the hospital in Loup City and they would take her there.

"What happened to him?" she asked. "Did he drown?"

"We'll explain on the way, ma'am," the deputy said.

Bonnie turned back into her bedroom and began untying her robe. The deputies discreetly retreated to the living room while she threw on a T-shirt, a pair of jeans and flip-flops.

On the drive to Loup City, the deputies explained that Curtis had been ambushed at the creek by ten or more boys and beaten to death. They left out the goriest of the details. However, they told her that the dispatch center received two separate 911 calls around one o'clock in the morning reporting that a boy had been badly injured at Mud Creek in Hazard.

"The callers were specific about the location, so we knew exactly where to go," the deputy in the passenger seat said as he looked back at Bonnie in the back seat.

"But by the time the paramedics got there he was barely alive and died on the way to the hospital," the other deputy said, anticipating Bonnie's question.

Throughout the narrative, Bonnie maintained her composure. Despite what they were saying, she couldn't bring herself to fully believe that her precious son was gone.

But when they led her into the hospital operating room, and she saw the shroud-covered body lying on the table, her resolve began to crumble. A doctor stood on the side of the head of the table with his hand on the sheet covering Curtis' head.

"Are you ready?" a deputy, standing behind Bonnie, softly asked.

She hesitated a moment and took a couple of deep breaths, then nodded. The deputy gently nudged her forward and once she was right next to the table opposite the doctor, he lifted the sheet to expose only Curtis' head. He was careful to hold the sheet in such a way that Bonnie could not see the head wound on his left side.

While there were some bruises around his eyes and mouth, there was no mistaking that it was Curtis. Bonnie felt her knees go weak, and her eyes began to water. The deputy stepped forward to help support her as she stood.

"Is that your son, Ms. Herden?" he whispered in her ear.

She tried to speak, but the words would not come out, so she nodded her head yes. The doctor quickly replaced the sheet over Curtis' lifeless head.

"You can stay with him for a few minutes if you like," the doctor said sympathetically.

Bonnie reached out and grabbed her son's cold hand underneath the sheet, held it for a moment, gave it one last squeeze then turned to leave the room. The deputies and doctor followed her into the hallway, where she sat in a chair and hung her head.

"How did he die?" she asked without lifting her head.

"We'll need to do an autopsy to know for sure," the doctor answered professionally.

Bonnie looked up and locked eyes with the doctor. Her gaze was so cold it could have put hell into a deep freeze.

"Did you examine him?" she threw the words at him.

"Yes, I did," he responded defensively.

"Then what do you think killed him?" she shot back.

After a brief hesitation, the doctor responded.

"There were wounds on the left side of his head and the back of his skull that indicated severe blunt force trauma, and there was a scalp wound that caused a great loss of blood," he said coldly.

Not entirely satisfied with the answers the doctor had given her, but sure she would not get anything more, Bonnie stood up and told the deputies she wanted to be taken home.

"I expect to be updated on the autopsy and the investigation into who did this to my son," she said loudly as she walked down the hallway as the tears began to flow. The deputies quick-stepped to keep up with her.

Bonnie called Lauralei as the deputies drove her back to Hazard. After they shared a good cry, Lauralei called Holly Quarters. She helped arrange some time off work for Lauralei and the two were in Holly's car within hours headed for Hazard.

While they were on the road, Holly called the Sherman County Sheriff's Office and the hospital in Loup City. She informed them she was Bonnie's lawyer and the advocate for Curtis. She tried to get as much information as she could, to be a conduit between law enforcement and medical and the mother of the dead boy.

Sheriff's deputies were by then rounding up and questioning all the boys who had been involved in the attack on Curtis. They had about half in the sheriff's office, including the two who had made the 911 calls. Because they had called the emergency line, the dispatcher insisted they give their names. When they were initially contacted by sheriff's deputies and learned the severity of the situation, they gave up the names of the other boys involved.

Sheriff Bradley Stein told Holly the explanations they were getting so far were varied in the details, but the basic story was the same. The group of boys had gone to Hazard to try and force Curtis to tell them where the missing girl was and what he had done to her. They claimed their understanding from the ringleader was that they would not physically harm Curtis. They simply counted on the overwhelming numbers and showed force to make him reveal the information they were looking for.

However, things escalated, and Curtis was physically attacked. The boys being questioned were reluctant to indicate how the affair got out of hand. But when threatened with being tried as adults for premeditated murder, their parents convinced them to admit the incident's ringleader not only ramped up the violence against Curtis; he was the one who delivered what the doctor speculated were the lethal blows to the head.

That ringleader was identified as Gerry Kline.

"You said this attack happened at a creek some distance from Curtis' house," Holly said, using the Bluetooth in her car so Lauralei could hear the whole conversation, as she zoomed down Interstate-80. "Did this gang of kids abduct Curtis and take him there?"

"That is a little unclear. We haven't found this Gerry Kline yet, so we haven't gotten his side of the story," the sheriff said. "But one of the kids we did talk to said Kline had surveilled

Curtis and the missing girl - Ruth Jung, but she is known as Mary - going to that spot at the creek."

"This was planned out in advance," Holly said, some anger creeping into her voice.

"It does appear that way," Stein said. "But we still haven't gotten the whole story yet."

Holly's next call was to the hospital and a short conversation with the doctor Bonnie had spoken with. He said the autopsy was scheduled for later in the afternoon.

"But even then, I can't share any information with you, only his mother and the police," the doctor said.

"I am the mother's attorney, and you will share that information with me because I will be the connection between you and the mother," Holly said bitterly. "When I get to Loup City, I'll get a court order that will compel you to do so."

The doctor started to protest, but Holly ended the call before he could get more than one word out. She then called Bonnie and explained all she had learned and told her all information about the case would flow through her.

"With your permission, of course," Holly quickly added.

Bonnie gladly gave her consent. Curtis' death was taking a toll on her, and she was not sure how long she could keep her cool in the face of law enforcement and the medical community. Besides, she had learned enough about Holly in her previous dealings with her that she could be a pit bull if necessary, much more than she herself could be even under the best of circumstances.

Once Lauralei and Holly arrived at Bonnie's home, there was a period of mourning and grief. Bonnie and Lauralei shared some memories of the boy, and Holly, who had the least contact with him, was saddened that she had not had more of a chance to get to know him.

Shortly after the stories about Curtis ran their course, there was a knock at Bonnie's door. Joachim and Ava Jung had come to offer their condolences, despite still being wracked with worry over their daughter's absence and uncertain fate.

Holly offered to help the Jungs in any way she could under the same pro bono arrangement she had with Bonnie.

"I believe I recall Curtis mentioned you had an older son," Bonnie said. "Does he know that Mary is missing?"

"It is not likely. He is serving in the German navy, and we have not been able to contact him. When we call, it does not connect. Perhaps his ship is at sea," Joachim said. "We have tried to get him a message through the Deutsche Marine, but all we get so far is what you Americans call red tape."

"Maybe that is where I can help," Holly said. "Let me make some calls, and I'll see what I can do through our State Department."

The Jungs gratefully agreed, giving Holly their son's name and the name of the ship to which he was assigned, as well as their cell phone numbers.

The Jungs then gave Bonnie a tight, warm hug.

"Our Mary talked about your Curtis often, and with affection," Ava said as the embrace ended. "I believe there were some deep feelings between them."

Lauralei, who had been able to get ten days off work to give her time to spend with Bonnie and attend any services planned for Curtis, stayed at Bonnie's in his bedroom. Bonnie offered Holly her room, but she would have none of it.

"I'm not going to put you out of your own room," she said with conviction.

While she agreed to stay at Bonnie's home, she slept on the couch -- when she slept at all. She planned to spend a lot of the daytime hours in Loup City badgering the sheriff's office for information on the case. When in Hazard - day or night - she spent her time on the phone keeping up to date on her cases in Wyoming, trying to track down Erich Jung and calling media outlets using Hazard as the epicenter and working her way outwards spreading the word about the missing girl.

The day after Lauralei and Holly arrived from Wyoming, Bonnie was forced to begin the unpleasant task of preparing for the final disposition of Curtis' body. Holly was able to get the information that an autopsy had been completed, so the body was to be released soon.

The cause of death, according to the report Holly obtained from the sheriff, was what the doctor had speculated at the hospital - blunt force trauma to the head and heavy blood loss. The report also stated Curtis had heavy bruising all over his torso and some on his arms and legs. The doctor estimated the wounds were sustained at around eleven o'clock at night, and Curtis likely lost consciousness within seconds of the head blows. However, the doctor projected he did not die until about three hours after the initial blows had been delivered. The doctor's report also speculated that Curtis' swollen brain likely stopped functioning fairly quickly after the head strikes, but the heart continued to pump blood until the ambulance was on its way to the hospital.

"Does that mean that if those kids hadn't waited almost two hours to make those 911 calls, he might have survived?" Holly had asked the sheriff.

"Maybe," he responded. "But there is no way to know for sure. Those times in the autopsy report are only estimates."

Holly decided to delay giving that bit of news to Bonnie. She needed to focus on the preparations for Curtis.

Bonnie initially wanted to bury her son on her Hazard property. But Nebraska law requires burials on private residential property to be supervised by a licensed funeral director. With Mary still missing, the sentiment among the public in the county was leaning toward Curtis as a suspect in her disappearance, even though he was dead. The first two morticians Bonnie contacted refused participation, fearing public backlash.

So, she opted for cremation and a private memorial service on her property. She, Lauralei and Holly traveled to Raveena, about eight miles away, to make the arrangements at a facility there. While returning to Hazard, Holly received a call from the Loup City hospital that Curtis' body would be released the following day. She gave the name of the crematorium, then called officials at that facility to let them know.

Once back at Bonnie's home, the trio of women began making plans for the memorial service. They had just begun when there was a knock at the front door.

Chapter 25

Holly, who had just come out of the kitchen, put out her hand to motion Bonnie back to her seat on the couch.

"I'll get this," she said.

She opened the main door.

"Is Curtis here?" came from outside.

The blood drained from Bonnie's face and, even though she wasn't looking in her direction or touching her in any way, Lauralei could feel her friend's entire body go taut with tension. Lauralei assumed it was because she had heard someone say Curtis' name. But she could tell there was more to it than that.

Bonnie jumped up and hurried to the door as she heard Holly tell the questioner, "He is not." Before she could say more, Bonnie was at her side, her mouth agape in shock. She felt dizzy, and she tried to speak, but the words got stuck in her throat. She reached to the side and took Holly's arm to steady herself. Seeing Bonnie's reaction, Lauralei jumped up and joined her friend.

Standing on her porch on the other side of the screen door was Mary. Behind her was a tall, stocky man wearing what appeared to be a military uniform, but Bonnie did not recognize it as American military.

They all saw the couple standing on the porch. The woman, dressed in jeans, sneakers and a long-sleeved blouse, looked puzzled.

"I want to introduce Curtis to someone," Mary said haltingly. "And to you," she added quickly.

"You can't," was all Bonnie could manage.

"Why not?" Mary asked.

"Who are you?" Holly asked before Bonnie could explain.

"It's Mary," Bonnie choked out.

"The missing girl?" Lauralei asked.

Holly reached forward and pushed up the hook lock on the screen door and pushed it open, motioning the two inside.

"I am Leutnant sur See Erich Jung, her brother," the man said, extending his hand.

The three women shook it in turn, but all staring at Mary the entire time.

"Why can't I introduce my brother to Curtis and you?" Mary asked.

"Because he's dead," Lauralei blurted out.

Bonnie began to sob as Mary stood and looked from her to the other women. Confusion and shock fell like a curtain down her face. Her brother took hold of her shoulders.

Lauralei guided Bonnie to the couch, and Holly invited Mary and Erich to sit in the two chairs.

"Do your parents know you are here?" Holly asked.

"We just got to town and wanted to come here first," Mary stammered, still trying to grasp the reality of what she had just been told.

"Call them now," Holly ordered.

While they waited for the Jungs to arrive, Holly told Mary and Erich all that had happened since she had turned up missing. When she got to the point of revealing what happened to Curtis, Mary broke down and cried heavily. Hearing it all over again also brought Bonnie to tears anew.

It was at precisely that time that the Jungs arrived. Lauralei ushered them inside and left them to spend a few minutes with their children. Taking advantage of the lull, Holly called the sheriff's office to notify them that Mary had turned up alive and well.

"Where have you been, Schatzchen," Ava asked. "We have been looking all over for you. We thought you were hurt, or worse." She couldn't bring herself to say the word dead. But her eyes filled with tears at the thought of it.

Still reeling from the news of Curtis' death, Mary could not get any words to come out.

"She had gone to New York, where my ship was docked," Erich said to fill the void.

"Why didn't we know this? Why didn't you tell us?" Joachim asked, looking from Mary to Erich.

"I had told Mary several weeks ago that the Bayern, my ship, would be in New York for two months for some modernization," he explained. "I was able to arrange a few weeks' leave and wanted to come and visit. I wanted to surprise you, so I told Mary not to say anything."

"Why did you go to New York?" Joachim asked his daughter. "And why do it in secret?"

"I wanted to see Erich alone before he came, and I didn't want to give away his surprise," she responded, finally finding her voice. "I didn't even tell Erich I was going to New York."

"How did you get there?" Ava asked.

"I hitchhiked to Litchfield and rode the bus to Grand Island and flew from there," she said sheepishly. Her mother gasped when she heard the word "hitchhiked."

"Where did you get money for a plane ticket?" her father asked.

"I had some money saved, and I borrowed some from Curtis," she said. As his name left her lips, she began to cry again.

"He said nothing to me about this," Bonnie said from the kitchen in answer to the Jung parents' inquiring looks.

"I never told him what the money was for, and he never asked," Mary said between sobs.

Bonnie went to answer a knock at the door, and the conversation paused. She found the same two sheriff's deputies and Sheriff Stein waiting on the porch. She invited them inside. She explained that they were hearing Mary's explanation of where she had been, and she quickly reviewed what had been revealed so far.

"I think it might be best if we interviewed Ms. Jung privately," the sheriff said. "With her parents present, of course."

Mary became frightened and moved closer to her mother, who put her arms around her daughter. Holly, who had come back into the living room, picked up on this right away.

"With all due respect, sheriff, I think it would be better if we continued in this format," the attorney said. "I am acting as attorney for everyone in this room." She looked at the Jungs for approval, and Joachim nodded. "And I believe you will get more detailed information if Mary and Erich, her brother, feel comfortable."

The sheriff gave his consent, then with prompting from Holly and her parents, Mary explained that she and Curtis had met late in the evening the previous Wednesday and gone to the creek. They talked for a while, then when Curtis suggested they go home, she had instructed him to go ahead.

"I didn't tell him that I was going to Litchfield to get on the bus," she said. "He would never have let me hitchhike."

Mary did not divulge the content of their conversation at the creek. But she then explained that after about fifteen minutes, she got up to begin her trek, but someone came out of the trees and walked toward her. It was Gerry Kline.

"He said I shouldn't be with Curtis. I should be with him," Mary said with disgust in her voice. "Then he grabbed me and tried to kiss me."

She gave him a shove but couldn't break his hold. He then began pulling her jacket off. She resisted, but he was able to get it off, and he tossed it aside. It landed in the water and began to float downstream. Mary said he then tried to pull up her T-shirt.

"That's when I kneed him in the crotch - twice," she said proudly.

Gerry doubled over in pain, releasing his hold on her. She bolted for the trees and the highway beyond. She kept running across the bridge, not even looking back until she got to where Highway 10 and Highway 2 met on the north end of town. She glanced over her shoulder and saw that Gerry was not following her. She slowed her pace, but kept jogging to her house. She grabbed the backpack she had prepared for the trip, hid under her bedroom window, and headed back to the highway.

As she walked slowly, keeping within the shadows in case Gerry had gone back to find her, she saw his pickup truck turn from one highway to the other and head north toward Litchfield. When she could no longer see his taillights, she began walking along the same highway in the same direction.

"I hadn't gone far when I got a ride from a nice woman who took me to Litchfield and dropped me off at the bus station," Mary concluded.

During her narrative, the deputies had taken copious notes. The sheriff whispered to one of them, and he left the house.

"And then you went to New York to see your brother, and then you both came back here," the sheriff said. "Did you fly back?"

"No. I was able to rent a car, and we drove," Erich said. "We stopped in Chicago and stayed the night."

"Are you going to be staying with your parents?" the sheriff asked. Erich nodded. "We'll need to be able to know where you are in case we have other questions." He nodded again.

"But I'll have to be back in New York in two weeks," Erich said.

The sheriff acknowledged that and the house fell quiet for a minute or two.

"So what is the latest on finding the people who did this to Curtis?" Holly broke the silence.

"We have ten of them in custody, and we're getting pretty much the same story from all of them," the sheriff said. "It appears the only one left to find is Gerry Kline."

He stood and motioned the other deputy to do the same.

"We will keep you posted if anything else develops," he told Holly, then turned to the rest of the people in the room. "Again, Ms. Herden, I am very sorry for your loss. And I am also pleased that Mary turned up safe and sound."

Holly followed the two law enforcement officers out the door. Mary got up and knelt in front of Bonnie.

"I am so sorry about what happened to Curtis," she said, beginning to cry again. "I really liked your son. He was very kind to me."

Bonnie patted her hand and said a quiet thank you. But there was a part of her that blamed Mary for the loss of her son. She couldn't shake the belief that if she had not disappeared, those boys would not have beaten him to death.

However, deep down, she knew it was not Mary's fault. Although he had not told her every detail, from what Curtis had shared with her about the bullying he received from Gerry and others, she was certain that was the root of it. It was likely a violent confrontation between Curtis and Gerry, either alone or with the same group of allies, would eventually happen. She would have to reconcile that in her own mind, but it was going to take some time.

Sheriff's deputies had gone to the Kline home, visited Hank Kline and Irene Kline at their jobs and officials at the high school trying to locate Gerry. They all claimed they had not seen him since that early morning when Curtis' lifeless body had been found next to Mud Creek.

His parents were concerned that something had happened to him as well, and suggested deputies look into Bonnie Herden. They had heard the stories and exaggerated gossip about what happened in Wyoming and the discovery of more than twenty-five thousand dollars in her pickup truck. They suggested she blamed Gerry for her son's death and had taken some kind of revenge.

Based on their interviews with the other ten boys who participated in the ambush and attack of Curtis, investigators had another theory. Because the Klines refused to give consent for a search of their property, deputies were simply waiting for a search warrant to be granted.

When they had it in hand, they searched the house and work shed thoroughly with no results. But when they opened the door of the root cellar, they found Gerry shivering among the potatoes, turnips and other vegetables grown in the Klines' garden then stored there. With the junk food containers, some opened and some not, and the sleeping bag, it was clear he had been there at least overnight, maybe for two nights.

Gerry was too cold and out of breath from being in the musty hole for so long to put up much resistance when deputies took him into custody and snapped on the handcuffs, deliberately snapping them as tight around his wrists as they would go.

Initially, during the drive to the Loup City courthouse and in his first hour of questioning, Gerry said nothing in response. Because he had recently turned eighteen, there was no requirement to have his parents present during the interrogation. Under the increasingly aggressive questioning by detectives, Gerry finally began to speak, but only to continually deny he had been involved in Curtis' death.

Deputies had read Gerry his Miranda rights when they cuffed him in front of the root cellar, but he was apparently not bright enough to invoke his right to have an attorney present - at least in the beginning. When he finally declined to say anything else without an attorney, there was a break in the action while they waited for a public defender. Deputies took the opportunity to have someone else brought to the courthouse.

Once Gerry and his lawyer had a chance to briefly confer, the questioning continued. Gerry continued to deny he had even been in Hazard on the night in question.

"We have ten eyewitnesses who put you at the scene," one detective said.

"They're lying to cover their asses," Gerry snarled.

"All ten of them? I find that hard to believe," the detective said.

"Sure. Why wouldn't they? They have to blame someone else for what they did," Gerry said.

The two detectives looked at each other.

"When was the last time you were in Hazard?" the second detective asked.

"I don't remember," Gerry muttered.

"We have information that puts you there several consecutive nights within the last two weeks," the first detective said.

"That's not true," Gerry growled.

The detectives ignored the response and plowed on.

"We further have information that says you were there to watch Curtis Herden and Ruth Jung to map out their activities," the second detective said.

"Who the hell is Ruth Jung?" Gerry snapped.

"She goes by Mary, as you well know," the detective said, and quickly went on as Gerry tried to respond. "You wanted to see where they went when they snuck out of their homes at night."

"Why the fuck would I care about that?" Gerry asked, a little hesitation creeping into his voice.

Recognizing the crack in his facade, the detectives bored in like a heavy-duty drill bit into a steel beam.

"You were setting up your ambush," the second detective said. "You blamed him for Mary's rejection of your sexual advances, and you wanted to get even."

"That's not why..." Gerry began, but caught himself at the same time his lawyer put a hand on his arm to stop him.

"Why what?" the detective stood up and leaned across the table with his hands supporting him with his face within a foot of Gerry's. This time he said nothing.

"You resented the time Mary spent with Curtis. You wanted her for yourself," the first detective rejoined the questioning, taking the same position as his partner.

"That's bullshit," Gerry said weakly.

Now, the detectives smelled blood in the water.

"In fact, you were there at Mud Creek the night Mary disappeared," the first detective said.

"No, I wasn't," Gerry said.

"Yes, you were. And after Curtis left Mary there, you came out of hiding and confronted her." The second detective said, raising his voice, as the detectives were now taking turns. The lawyer started to protest, but he was ignored.

"Not true," Gerry said with forced conviction.

"It is true. And you tried to kiss her, and she rejected you." Gerry shook his head. "That made you mad, and you tried to force yourself on her." He shook his head more. "You tried to take her clothes off."

"That didn't happen. You're making it up," Gerry yelled, almost crying.

"Oh, it happened. Mary told us herself," the first detective said.

"She couldn't have," Gerry sputtered. "She's gone. That asshole Curtis probably killed her."

Both detectives eased back from the table with satisfying smiles curling their lips. The trap was ready to be sprung. The second detective turned, looked at the two-way mirror and nodded. The door to the interview room opened, and Mary stepped inside, escorted by a deputy.

Gerry's face went as white as a mime's. He sat in his chair, staring at her for nearly a full minute. Just as the color started to return to his face, the second detective gave the escorting deputy a small wave, and she and Mary left the room.

"Now, let's get down to what really happened," the first detective said as he and his partner sat down.

Chapter 26

Bonnie Herden sat in one of the wooden lawn chairs in her front yard. It was now the middle of June, nearly three months since Curtis' death and the aftermath that rocked half of Sherman County.

She looked across at another of the chairs, where her only child might have been sitting that Saturday, enjoying the crisp, motionless air that summer afternoon. She asked herself again how she had managed to piece her life back together after the horrific events that took her son away from her. The sounds and smell of the hay being cut in the adjoining field tugged at her grief. Curtis had spent hours watching the operation and then finally helped work the field himself.

"He would have been a great farmer," Bonnie whispered to herself, wiping away the tears that had rolled down her cheeks.

The past week was her first back to work at the county courthouse in Loup City. Her supervisors had been very generous, allowing her to take as much time as she needed to mourn her loss. But two weeks ago, she had had enough solitude. Sitting around at home thinking about Curtis and how much she missed him for the past two months had dulled her senses and kept her depressed. She needed activity and things to sharpen her mind.

The memorial service for Curtis, conducted within days of his death, was a simple affair conducted in the backyard. All four Jungs attended, along with Lauralei, Holly, Bonnie and three of her colleagues from the courthouse. A minister from the Hazard church recited a few passages from the Bible, then departed. The other attendees stayed at the house for several hours sharing memories about Curtis and half-heartedly partaking of potluck dishes that had been brought.

Lauralei could not stay longer than the original ten days allotted. Her boss wanted her to return to work, and she needed to keep her job. Since Holly had driven her to Hazard, she bought Lauralei a plane ticket to return. After Lauralei had to return to Wyoming for work, Holly had stayed for a month. She wanted to stay to continue to be a thorn in the side of the sheriff's and district attorney's office to get the best justice for Curtis. But she, too, had to eventually return to Wyoming. She had her own cases there to oversee. Bonnie promised to keep her updated.

Even without Holly's prodding, the legal case against the eleven boys who attacked Curtis moved along quickly and smoothly. The arraignment testimony from the ten other boys at Mud Creek about the events there and what Gerry had told them about his surveillance of Curtis and Mary made for a clear-cut case of premeditated murder. Mary's testimony about

Gerry's attempted sexual advances on her the night she disappeared, and his threatening behavior toward her that day at the high school when Curtis came to her aid, added more fuel to the prosecution's fire.

Gerry's attorney eventually convinced him to make a plea deal to avoid the death penalty. He pled guilty to second-degree murder. The other boys also made plea deals to assault and battery.

The wielder of the pipe that delivered the third blow to Curtis' head was never identified.

The plea deals did not set well with Bonnie, or Holly when she got the news. They both believed justice had not been adequately served, with all circumstances considered. But there was little they could do until the sentencing, scheduled for late in July, when the family and others could give their impact statements.

At that time, Mary and Bonnie were the only two to speak at the hearing for Gerry Kline.

"Curtis Herden was my friend," Mary began, facing the judge. She could not bring herself to look at Gerry. "He was my very best friend."

She paused for a moment to collect her thoughts. She had not prepared a statement on paper, preferring to speak from the heart.

"Curtis was a very kind boy. He would not have intentionally hurt anyone. Yes, there were instances when he lashed out. But those were in response to bullying directed at him. And I can tell you it took a lot to bring him to the point of lashing out," Mary said.

Again, she paused to wipe tears from her eyes.

"I know this because Curtis and I spent a lot of time together talking about many things. We had a special place where we walked and talked. Now that special place has been spoiled because that is where a gang of mean-spirited bullies beat my best friend to death," Mary said. "I loved Curtis Herden. We could have been more than friends, we could have had a future together. But now, because of those criminals, that will never happen."

Her emotions caught up with her and she hesitated to try and get them under control.

"You should be put to death, but because of the cowardly bully that you are, that won't happen," Mary blurted.

Afraid she would break down if she tried to say anything further, she left the podium, making sure her back was to Gerry.

Bonnie had no such desire to avoid facing her son's killer. She walked to the podium and turned to glare at Gerry. He tried to avoid looking at her. She had prepared a written statement, but when he avoided her gaze, she went off script.

"You would look away, you piece of crap. Because you are nothing but a bully, and all bullies are cowards," she said. "You couldn't face my son alone; you had to get as many others as you could to help you kill him. That makes you an even more pathetic coward."

Gerry slowly looked toward her and scowled.

"My son was not a filthy coward like you. And he was none of the things you called him since we moved to Hazard. Curtis was a good man, a very gentle soul. He did not deserve to die. And he certainly did not deserve to die at the hands of a bunch of damned stinking bastard cowards," Bonnie said.

She could feel the anger boiling up in her veins. All she wanted to do was rush to the table where Gerry, dressed in his orange jumpsuit rather than the suit and tie he had worn at the arraignment, and strangle him with her bare hands. But she knew if she did that she would be no better than he was. Besides, the bailiffs would stop her before she could finish the job.

"For what you did to my Curtis, you deserve to die. But because you are such a coward, this court can't make that happen. My only hope is that when you get to prison, a bunch of big burly guys give you everything you gave my son, you slimy piece of shit," Bonnie said, then stormed back to her seat, shooting daggers at Gerry the whole way.

At the hearing for the others, Mary gave a similar statement to what she did at Gerry's. Bonnie's statement was toned down a bit, but still laced with the word coward.

The judge sentenced Gerry to twenty years to life in prison, but he would be eligible for parole. The other ten participants in the assault were sentenced to 15 years in prison with the possibility of parole in at least five years.

As with the changes, Bonnie was disappointed with the penalties, and she left no doubt in anyone's mind in the courtroom how she felt.

"There is no real justice in Nebraska," she shouted when the judge's gavel banged at the end of his statement.

Shortly after Lauralei and Holly returned to Wyoming, Bonnie received a phone call one Sunday afternoon from Mary, who asked if she could come to the house and talk with her. Bonnie agreed.

While Bonnie had assigned some blame to Mary for Curtis' death, she never severed contact with the girl or her parents. Ava called her almost weekly to see how she was doing, and Bonnie always spoke to her politely. Mary walked by the house from time to time in the evenings, and when Bonnie was outdoors and saw her, she always returned Mary's waves. But they never spoke.

When Mary arrived that Sunday, Bonnie invited her into the house, and they sat together on the couch. The gold-plated urn that contained Curtis' ashes was the only item on the coffee table in front of them. They both stared at it uncomfortably for a few seconds.

"I wanted to tell you again how sorry I am about Curtis," Mary finally said awkwardly. "If I hadn't taken off without telling anyone, he would still be alive."

Bonnie had actually had the same thought many times over the last three months. But she suddenly felt a wave of guilt fill her soul.

"No, Mary, you don't know that," Bonnie heard herself saying.

"But those boys did that to him because they thought he did something to me," Mary said.

"That Gerry Kline has been bullying Curtis since we moved here. I'm sure he told you about that," Bonnie said. "It kept getting worse, and I'm sure it would have come to a head on its own."

"But..." Mary began, but Bonnie took her hands, stopping her before she could get started.

"Boys like Gerry Kline can get others worked up into a frenzy very easily, especially if they are followers, which these boys clearly are," Bonnie said. "You had nothing to do with that gang making the terrible decisions they did."

Mary looked down at Bonnie's hands holding hers. They were soft and gentle against her skin.

"You cared very much for my son; I could see that," Bonnie said. "There is no way you could have done anything to harm him, intentionally or otherwise."

Mary was overcome by Bonnie's words and began to cry. Bonnie pulled the young woman toward her and gathered her into a tight hug. They remained embraced for several minutes until Mary's sobs subsided. When they separated, they both glanced at the urn on the table.

"I think having his ashes will help give you comfort," Mary whispered.

"Actually, I have been thinking about that lately," Bonnie said after a moment's pause. "It has been a comfort. But I also think it's been too much of a reminder that he's no longer here."

Mary gave her a puzzled look.

"I need to move on," Bonnie explained. "I think Curtis would want me to."

"What would you do with them? Wouldn't you want to keep them?" Mary asked.

"Curtis wanted to be a farmer, as I'm sure you know. I have been thinking of spreading his ashes in the field next to our property. He worked there. I think he would like it," Bonnie explained.

She then reached under the end table and grabbed her purse. She reached in and pulled out two glass vials about the size of sewing thimbles. They were attached to small, delicate necklaces and were filled with gray material.

"The crematorium offered one of these, and I asked for two," Bonnie said. "At the time, I didn't know why I asked for two, but now I do."

She handed one of them to Mary. She knew instantly what was in the vials. She held it tight to her chest.

"Thank you, Ms. Herden," she said, choking back a few tears.

The women sat in silence for a few minutes.

"Won't you need to get permission from the owner to spread Curtis' ashes in his field?" Mary asked.

"What he doesn't know won't hurt him," Bonnie answered.

On Bonnie's insistence Mary stayed until after dark. Then the two crossed into the field that Curtis had watched so intently from his yard then cut and baled hay there. They waded through the waist-high hay to the center of the circular field. They stood for a few moments facing east. They could see the Farmall tractor and cutter parked on the far edge. The first cutting would begin the following morning.

Then Bonnie took the stopper from the urn and, moving from one side to the other, let half the ashes fall from the vessel. Some fell quickly to the ground, while some caught the slight breeze and floated over the green carpet of hay. Bonnie handed the urn to Mary, who turned back toward the house and scattered the remainder in the same manner.

Curtis Herden was now where he wanted to be.

About the Author

Rusty Bradshaw has been around. Born in California, grew up in Wyoming, spent many years in Oregon, now in Arizona. After graduating from Dubois High School in Wyoming, he attended Northwest College in Powell, Wyoming then went to Oregon to obtain his bachelor's degree from Eastern Oregon University. It was in Oregon where Rusty, an avid reader, started what has been a 40-plus year career in journalism at several newspapers in Seaside, St. Helens, Milton-Freewater and Astoria. During his career in Oregon, Rusty won several writing awards from the Oregon Newspaper Publishers Association. He was also named Junior Citizen of the Year by the Milton-Freewater Chamber of Commerce and coached youth football for nine years.

Rusty's career continued after a move to Arizona in 2004. He was editor of two newspapers in age-restricted communities – Sun City and Sun City West. He has two grown children – Sara in Oregon and Evan in Idaho. He lives in Glendale with his wife, Jeanne, who has a grown son – Billy, in Arizona. They enjoy football, bingo, road trips, jigsaw puzzles and any other activities they can do together. Rusty is also a photographer with a large portfolio of scenics for sale.

Printed in the USA
CPSIA information can be obtained
at www.ICGtesting.com
CBHW071948070324
5042CB00002B/5

9 781917 096713